MN

303277911 9

KU-146-592

AB

Born and raised on the Wirral Peninsula in England, **Charlotte Hawkes** is mum to two intrepid boys who love her to play building block games with them and who object loudly to the amount of time she spends on the computer. When she isn't writing—or building with blocks—she is company director for a small Anglo/French construction firm. Charlotte loves to hear from readers and you can contact her at her website: charlotte-hawkes.com.

Also by Charlotte Hawkes

The Army Doc's Secret Wife
The Surgeon's Baby Surprise
A Bride to Redeem Him
The Surgeon's One-Night Baby

Hot Army Docs miniseries

Encounter with a Commanding Officer
Tempted by Dr Off-Limits

Discover more at millsandboon.co.uk.

CHRISTMAS WITH HER BODYGUARD

CHARLOTTE HAWKES

MILLS & BOON

All rights reserved including the right of reproduction in whole or in part in any form. This edition is published by arrangement with Harlequin Books S.A.

This is a work of fiction. Names, characters, places, locations and incidents are purely fictional and bear no relationship to any real life individuals, living or dead, or to any actual places, business establishments, locations, events or incidents. Any resemblance is entirely coincidental.

This book is sold subject to the condition that it shall not, by way of trade or otherwise, be lent, resold, hired out or otherwise circulated without the prior consent of the publisher in any form of binding or cover other than that in which it is published and without a similar condition including this condition being imposed on the subsequent purchaser.

® and TM are trademarks owned and used by the trademark owner and/or its licensee. Trademarks marked with ® are registered with the United Kingdom Patent Office and/or the Office for Harmonisation in the Internal Market and in other countries.

First published in Great Britain 2018
by Mills & Boon, an imprint of HarperCollins*Publishers*
1 London Bridge Street, London, SE1 9GF

Large Print edition 2019

© 2018 Charlotte Hawkes

ISBN: 978-0-263-07827-5

MIX
Paper from
responsible sources
FSC   **FSC™ C007454**
www.fsc.org

This book is produced from independently certified FSC™ paper to ensure responsible forest management. For more information visit www.harpercollins.co.uk/green.

Printed and bound in Great Britain
by CPI Group (UK) Ltd, Croydon, CR0 4YY

To Mum,
for all the hats you wore!
You're my inspiration xxx

CHAPTER ONE

'REALLY, RAFE.' GRITTING her teeth to stay calm, Rae hurried behind her half-brother's long strides as he burned through the Rawlstone Group's UK headquarters. 'I appreciate you're only looking out for me, but I really don't need a bodyguard. Especially around Christmas.'

Her stomach roiled at the mere thought of another bodyguard. Even after all these years.

'I'm sorry, Rae.' He sounded genuinely regretful. 'If there were any other way...'

'There has to be,' she pleaded. 'Please, Rafe, you know the press will take any excuse to rake up the past. They never believed in my innocence as it was, and I couldn't bear it. Not again.'

Another stomach lurch. It was hard enough putting up with paparazzi dogging her daily life, pretending she didn't care what lies they wrote about her, or how little the public thought of her. She certainly didn't need to give them a reason to rerun all those stories of her utterly spectacular plummet into shame almost fourteen years ago.

No matter what she'd done to try to redeem herself, they had refused to believe that she'd known nothing about the sex tape, let alone leaked it. It had taken her ten years and a career in medicine to get them to finally stop linking her—usually scandalously—to every Hollywood A-lister, every rock musician, or every trust-fund kid in whose presence she was spotted.

It hadn't mattered that she'd barely even exchanged a word with some of them, let alone dated them. Sex sold. Scandal sold. That was all that mattered to them for so, so long. Only in the last four years had they finally, reluctantly, begun to come around to her side.

A bodyguard would undo all that good work. She could just read the headlines now.

Scarlet woman Raevenne Rawlstone finally takes a new bodyguard. Will he be as under-cover *as the last one?*

And that would be one of the tamer offerings.

Hot shame flooded her body as X-rated images, intimate moments that never had been anything but private, filled her brain.

'I can't have another bodyguard,' she choked out. 'I won't.'

Abruptly, her legs gave out and she just about made it to the wall for support, the old stonework rough beneath her hands. She'd trailed her fingers over their cool surface many times in the past, but tonight they seemed colder than usual, sapping her body heat as unseen edges cut into her skin. Rae withdrew her hand abruptly.

She usually loved visiting Rafe here. The offices might be as super high-tech as every other square millimetre of real estate in the company's portfolio, but Rafe's flair for restoring vast, old buildings, with their inspiring architecture, always had her gasping with admiration.

Today, however, she barely noticed the glorious stonework or vaulted ceilings. December was in a matter of weeks and yet she couldn't envisage the festive lights and decorations that would go transform this place into something infinitely magical. She didn't even think about the fact that, when the offices closed their proverbial business doors for the Christmas shutdown, Rafe would open the physical doors to the house and feed the homeless, the way he always did for those ten days.

Her half-brother was moving back to her,

reaching out to cup her shoulder, the closest he came to a hug. None of the Rawlstone clan found it easy to show emotion—an overhang from their mutual father, the cold and remote Ronald Rawlstone—but she and Rafe both knew they cared about each other.

'We'll deal with the press if we need to. You won't be alone, Rae. But I told you, I received a death threat the other day.'

'We always receive death threats.' She waved her hands desperately. 'We're Rawlstones.'

Or at least *her* side of the Rawlstone family always received death threats. Her limelight-loving sisters and mother had made it their mission with their *Life in the Rawl* reality show.

By contrast their half-brother, Rafe, CEO of the Rawlstone Group and former British army officer, was generally universally adored. At least by the press and public.

'This one is credible,' he replied simply. 'So, it's precisely because it *is* Christmas that I need to know you're safe. Especially with all the festive fundraisers and seasonal socials you'll no doubt be compelled to attend. Your sisters already have bigger personal protection details than even *they* need, as does your mother. It's *you* I worry about.'

She stared miserably at some fixed point on the stonework that her eyes didn't even see. 'They'll bring it all back up…what happened with Justin.'

The images flashed up again and she squeezed her eyes shut. It didn't help. She could still see it. The moment she'd lost her virginity played out on social media for the world to see.

She might have gagged, she couldn't be sure, but suddenly she was wrapped in a tight, if awkward, embrace.

'The guy was a piece of scum.' Controlled fury laced his voice along with a thread of guilt, and she hated that her half-brother felt even slightly responsible for the mistakes she'd made so many years ago. 'I'll never let anything like that happen to you again.'

'You can't promise that.' Her voice sounded more strained than she would have preferred.

'I can.' Releasing her slightly, Rafe took a step back. 'I personally requested the guy I've chosen to be our bodyguard. I trust him. He's a major from my army days.'

Her heart actually stopped beating for a moment.

And another.

It took everything she had to tell herself not to be so foolish. That it couldn't possibly *be*. And still her throat was thick, constricted, her tongue too big for her mouth, when she replied.

'He's some major or other from your army days?'

'Not *some* major,' Rafe disapproved. 'Myles is one of the best officers I had the pleasure to serve with.

Everything receded. Went black.

She had no idea how long she stood there but when she came back, squeezing her eyes closed, she was eternally grateful that Rafe was too busy marching along to have turned around to look at her.

There seemed little point in trying to soothe and corral her skittering heart but she made a valiant effort nonetheless.

'Myles.'

As if, perhaps, it could possibly be a different *Myles*.

'That's right, Major Myles Garrington.' She could practically hear Rafe's eye-roll. 'I mentioned it was him before. Keep up, Rae.'

'You didn't,' she managed feebly.

Myles. Numbness crept over her, but she had to hold herself together. Especially in front of Rafe. Her half-brother's opinion was the only one that mattered to her these days; she certainly couldn't let him know how she'd thrown herself at his best friend all those years ago.

She managed to stumble after him.

'Oh, well, no matter.' Rafe was oblivious. 'Myles is a decent bloke—you'll like him. You might not remember but you even met him once. He came with me the one and only Christmas holiday I spent with your family…oh, probably fifteen years ago now.'

Actually, fifteen years and two months ago. Not that she was counting. Much.

It was the only Christmas that Rafe had come to his half-family's home. It had been at their mutual father's insistence. As though the shocking death of his first wife had made Ronald Rawlstone suddenly remember the son he'd had little contact with—other than sending monthly financial support—for the best part of two decades.

She still didn't know why Rafe had agreed—duty, probably, her half-brother had a strong sense of duty—she only knew that he'd brought his best friend, a fellow junior army officer, with him.

Myles Garrington.

He had changed her life in so many ways. Not all of them good.

And how humiliating that the numbness was

only now beginning to recede because her traitorous body was already tingling at the memories of Myles that began to lace their way into her brain. Memories she'd spent fifteen years trying to bury.

The attraction between her and Myles when he'd walked into the Rawlstone family home with Rafe had been instantaneous. Its intensity had side-swiped her, and at seventeen—barely a few months off eighteen—it had been long overdue. Myles had just turned twenty-one, a medical student at uni, and already a junior officer in the British army. He'd seemed so much wiser and more mature than the American boys from her high school, and she'd fallen so very hard, so very fast. She'd genuinely believed him to be her first love. With the benefit of hindsight, of course, she recognised it for what it had really been...her first intense crush. Nothing more.

But still, when she looked back over that Christmas holiday she knew she'd acted wantonly. Then again, he hadn't exactly beaten her off him.

Except for that last night.

'Anyway,' the usually astute Rafe continued, his pace unrelenting, 'Myles was one of the best officers the British army had.'

'Had?'

A sense of foreboding crept over her. Being an army trauma doctor had been Myles' sole focus in life. She couldn't imagine him ever leaving of his own volition.

'He left six months ago.'

'Why?'

To most other people it would have been indiscernible, but Rae didn't miss Rafe's uncharacteristic beat of hesitation.

'There was a village. A fire. One of the riflemen protecting Myles' medical team…died. Myles was injured badly, too… His hand. He couldn't operate for a while but he couldn't stand the idea of getting stuck behind a desk. Possibly there was a degree of survivor's guilt, too. He'd been going through the process of coming to the States anyway so taking a clinical observation post under your supervision means he can still do that whilst also protecting you around the clock.'

'Round the clock?' She gasped. 'He can't live with me.'

'Do you want to stay safe, or would you prefer to pander to your sensibilities?'

'Rafe—'

'Relax.' He cut her off with a half-smile. 'I

don't mean to needle you. For the moment it seems this threat is UK-based, so he'll accompany you to your lecture tonight and on the private jet back to the States tomorrow. But he won't need to live with you… I've purchased the property next door.'

There was no reason for her to feel so panicked. No reason at all. And if there was, she told herself firmly, it was at the idea that people had been hurt. Not at the thought of being in Myles' company twenty-four seven.

'Wait, you said Myles was hurt?'

Clearly there was more to it than that but it was little comfort to know her instincts had been correct. Still, since Rafe hadn't stopped pounding along the corridors leaving Rae's legs burning as she tried to keep up, this wasn't going to be the ideal time to press him on it.

'Wind your neck in, Rae. I didn't say that.'

It was so far from Rafe's usual lexicon that there was no missing his agitation. Which perhaps helped to explain why he apparently hadn't noticed she'd gone from pretending not to remember Myles to showing fear he had been hurt.

Ironically, that only stirred her up all the more. Still, she needed to be more careful. More blasé.

'Wind my neck in?' She fought back her agitation to teasing him, shedding her American accent in order to imitate his vaguely plummy English pitch. 'My dear brother, I do believe you're the one who had me practically frog-marched from my thirty-six-hour shift at the hospital onto your private jet and flown across the Atlantic. Yet *I'm* the one who needs to "wind my neck in"?'

'Funny, Rae.' She could almost hear him roll his eyes at her. 'Your impersonation leaves a lot to be desired. You could take the Dick Van Dyke award for abysmal cockney accents. I'll warn Myles.'

She forced a laugh and told herself she wasn't getting anxious. She had to pretend that his existence meant absolutely nothing to her.

Which, of course, it did.

It was only galling that she didn't find herself remotely convincing.

'Fine.' She forced a dazzling grin even though her half-brother couldn't see her. 'You try my accent. I bet you can't sound like a New Yorker.'

'Rae,' he cautioned.

'Seriously, give it a try.'

'Raevenne.' He stopped at last, turning around to face her, his hands on her shoulders. 'Stop panicking.'

Her stomach somersaulted again. Her half-brother *knew*? Surely that was impossible.

She was only relieved she'd slept most of the plane journey and her shift at the hospital had been so busy that she hadn't eaten more than a biscuit for the last eighteen hours. At least it meant there was nothing to regurgitate.

'Who said I'm panicking?' Her shrill voice didn't help and she stopped abruptly.

The silence was practically pressing in on her as she nonetheless followed Rafe up the stairs to his office in the panoramic suite on the tenth floor. He never took an elevator if he could take the stairs. One of the few overhangs he couldn't conceal from his years in conflict zones as a frontline officer in the British army. Thank goodness for her own daily cardio sessions at the exclusive gym uptown.

And for the fact that they weren't in the Manhattan office with its sixty-five storeys.

Then, all too soon, they were standing in the anteroom to Rafe's office, her heart threatening to pound out of her chest at any moment.

Myles was on the other side of the door and she wasn't ready for this. She wasn't ready to face him. To see even a shadow of disgust or condemnation in his expression.

Rafe's hand reached for the door handle.

'I can't...' she choked out, stumbling backwards.

'Well, if you can't do it for yourself, or even for me, then do it for Myles, Rae. He'd never say it but I think he needs us. The firefight was bad, Rae, it took Myles out for months whilst he wasn't able to operate.'

A surgeon who couldn't operate? *Myles* unable to operate? It didn't bear thinking about.

She'd been ready for Rafe's cajoling, even for him to order her in. But she hadn't been prepared for him to lay such a perfect trap. It was her Achilles heel. If someone needed her help, she could never deny them. Rafe had known it, and he'd baited her shamelessly.

'What's going on, Rafe?' She glowered at him even as she was compelled to ask the question, but Rafe simply shook his head.

'It isn't my story to tell.'

Frustration rushed her, but she was determined to hold her nerve. At least, outwardly.

'If you want me to agree to this—' she was amazed she managed to make it sound as if she were actually in control—as though her body hadn't been turning itself inside out, caught between longing and sheer terror, from the moment she'd discovered that Myles was even in the building '—then you'll tell me exactly what's going on. Now.'

Myles could hear them, out in the corridor. Talking quietly.

He couldn't make out the words but the context was unmistakeable. The higher, female voice, clearly Rae's, was demanding. Rafe's deeper voice was firm but uncharacteristically urgent. Myles gripped the sides of the plush chair and shifted awkwardly.

Why the hell had he ever agreed to this?

An image of Raevenne hovered in the back of his mind but he pushed it easily aside.

Ridiculous.

He wasn't here for her. He was here because he had no other choice. Because he needed a job that took him away from battlefields and death, and Rafe, his former best friend, had offered him exactly that. And because his painstakingly constructed life had unravelled so incalculably these past six months.

Almost seventeen years in the British army— where he'd thought he would stay his whole life—over. Just like that.

Guilt pressed in on him.

Heavy.

Suffocating.

He blocked out the images—the smell of burning flesh, the village burned to the ground, young Lance Corporal Mike McCoy—which threatened to overwhelm him. Blackness closed over him and for a dangerous moment he swayed on the spot.

Only his subconscious fighting to lock on the familiar, feminine voice, muffled as it was through the door, provided him an anchor to the present.

He grasped at it gratefully.

One day at a time. Wasn't that the advice he'd given out, time and again over the years, to soldiers in his position? Never imagining that one day it would be him standing there, his life having imploded and now lying in tatters around him.

But this wasn't the army. Or what had happened *out there*. This was simple, uncomplicated, repaying an old debt to a good friend. Playing bodyguard whilst Rafe tracked down exactly who was threatening his family.

And right now, being a bodyguard beat being a surgeon hands down. True, part of Rafe's plan included clinical observation but he could handle that. Observation was one thing. It was staying an active surgeon right now that certainly wasn't an option.

An operating room with a body on the table in front of him and a scalpel in his hand was no place for a man who suspected he was on the edge of mild PTSD. His heart hammered angrily at the mere thought of it. At such an obvious sign of his own weakness. But those tours of duty had taken so many men and women he knew, so many innocent kids, so many helpless civilians, particularly that last week. And especially that last mission.

When perhaps he could have...*should* have... made different choices.

All those women, those kids. Mikey. It had taken them all.

Did it have to have taken part of his soul, too?

The sounds in the hallway provided a sudden, welcome distraction from his uncharacteristic moment of self-pity.

Ten operational tours in the past twelve years alone, sometimes back-to-back, and never once had he allowed himself to look back and dwell. Everybody knew that was the road to self-destruction because it wouldn't bring anybody back and it was a waste of time.

Galvanised, he pushed himself out of the seat and stalked across the floor just as the door swung open and the familiar form of his former army buddy strode in. But it was the figure slinking in behind Rafe—her head resolutely down—that arrested his gaze.

Raevenne Rawlstone.

He hadn't thought about her in years.

Liar.

He ignored the silent accusation.

But he *had* shoved memories of her, of that one Christmas together, to the back of his mind. Yet now, having heard Rae's muffled yet nevertheless unmistakeable voice through the door, he found he couldn't stuff her back into whatever cold corner of his mind in which she'd been lurking all these years.

It was insane. Objectionable. Unacceptable. And yet, it seemed, here he was.

He wasn't aware that he'd crossed the room towards her until she lifted her head—those unmistakeable laurel-green eyes with their perfect, moss-green edging that had haunted him far more than he had ever cared to admit—and finally met his stare full-on.

His breath lodged, as though he were winded, as though seeing her for the first time in fifteen years. Innocent and fragile. So far removed from those gossip columns, those entertainment channels, that awful *Life in the Rawl* reality show.

He'd tried to escape them but it hadn't been easy. When you were out in a conflict zone it was amazing what light escapism soldiers found entertaining. And still, it made him grit his teeth so hard he was surprised his jaw didn't break.

'Ma'am,' he ground out stiffly before his brain got into gear.

It was ridiculous given how they'd once known each other, and he wasn't surprised she hesitated before sliding her smaller palm against his and managing a stiff handshake.

'Major.'

Was that a jolt of...*something*...surging through him?

Impossible.

So why was he having to fight himself not to snatch his hand away?

Myles glanced back at her.

He had no words to articulate why he felt so upended. Or even what it was. Which was when she opened her mouth and bit out, 'I don't want you as my bodyguard.'

Not quite that fragile, then.

Something else tipped sideways within him

and suddenly, bizarrely, he found himself fighting a faint smile that toyed on his lips.

He thrust the odd sensation aside, reaching instead for his more familiar cloak of dispassion and finding something slightly less reassuring. It was all he could do to school his features.

'Something wrong?'

She cocked her head to the side as if actually contemplating it.

It occurred to him that he hadn't had anyone *evaluate* him like this in a long, long time. Ever since he'd been a desperate recruit, prepared to leopard crawl from Fort William to Cape Wrath if it meant winning an army bursary to study medicine.

'I think I might prefer someone who looks like they could handle a shoving, unruly crowd. Someone *more...*'

Belatedly, he realised she was deliberately trying to insult him.

'More?' He arched one eyebrow as though indulging a silly, petulant child, which, he reminded himself, was exactly how he saw her.

'Yes, you know, *more...*' She waved her hand airily. 'Bigger, more intimidating.'

'Is that so?'

'That's....so.' She flicked out her tongue and

the movement snagged his gaze. Inexplicably he couldn't seem to draw his eyes away.

'Indeed? Well, if you're worried that you aren't going to be…safe enough with me, I can assure you that I have no intention of letting anyone go near you.'

Including himself, he concluded haughtily, and it felt like an odd kind of triumph. Almost as if they were sparring again, the way they had done all those Christmases ago.

What the hell was going on, here?

'That aside,' she stated primly, 'are you always this high-handed and condescending? Or is it just because it's me?'

The flashes of the Raevenne he used to know weren't doing much to help his sense of self-control. Oddly, it was as if a light were suddenly glinting through him, casting tiny spots of illumination and colour on a darkness that had been growing for too long.

A part of him wanted to lean towards that light.

A bigger part of him wanted to extinguish it.

'Not usually. Then again, I don't often come across someone so infamously flippant and disparaging.'

She glowered at him, and instead of it confirming every last, negative rumour he'd ever heard, he found himself oddly drawn to her. Still, he held his ground.

He wasn't sure who was more startled when Rafe cut in, clearly amused.

'Glad you still remember how to handle my sister's prickly side.'

It was testament to how much his old friend thought of his half-sister that he dispensed with the *half* part of the title.

Interesting.

'Seems so.' Myles forced a lightness into his tone. He wasn't sure why, but he couldn't allow Rafe to see there was any issue between him and Rae.

'Good, then there's an urgent business call I really need to make. I'll see you both tonight at the conference. Good luck, Rae. I know your lecture will be incredible.'

Then Rafe was gone, leaving the two of them alone in the plush office suite.

For several long moments neither of them spoke.

'So,' Myles finally broke the silence, fighting the urge to clear his throat, 'you're a doctor now?'

CHAPTER TWO

HE HADN'T INTENDED the emphasis on *now*. Hadn't meant to sound so disparaging. But the storm raging in his head wasn't letting him think straight.

'I am. Obstetrics and gynaecology.' She lifted her head proudly and something kicked in his chest. 'And I'm a good one, too. I'm also a maternal and foetal medicine specialist.'

She was actually sparkling. That moss-green edging in her eyes seemed more like a deeper navy blue right now, which had always meant her emotions were running high. He'd learned to read Rae through her eyes long, long ago.

'So Rafe said.' He wrenched himself back to the present.

'Right.' She bit her lip and it did something to his gut that it had no business doing.

'He also told me you were giving a keynote speech at the World Precision Medicine Conference tonight.'

Her cheeks flushed again.

'I am. And I heard you gave a brilliant lecture there a few years ago. I was meant to attend but…there was a medical emergency and I missed my plane.'

She offered a rueful grin and suddenly it occurred to him that whatever stories the media told—however they touched on her medical career but focussed on her personal life—Rae was utterly invested in her career as a doctor.

This, Myles realised with a start, was more like the Raevenne he remembered from all those years ago.

The rest of the world might know her as the girl who had catapulted her despicable side of the Rawlstone family onto the reality scene with a sex tape of her eighteen-year-old self and her twenty-eight-year-old bodyguard.

But that wasn't the girl that he'd known. At least, not back then.

It wasn't the sweet, blushing seventeen-year-old with whom he'd felt an attraction from the moment Rafe had introduced them. He'd tried to fight it, of course—Rafe had been his best mate, but even at seventeen she'd seemed far older, far more mature, than her years. The three years between them had melted away and, cooped up in that house trying to stay away from the rest of Rafe's god-awful half-family—from the self-serving mother to the callous father so wretchedly similar to his own—he and Rae had forged a bond.

And then, despite his best intentions, the heady glances had evolved to fleeting touches, stolen kisses, and something so much more intense. He'd wanted her with such a ferocity, as he'd wanted no other woman before.

Probably as he'd wanted no other woman since, either.

It had taken a supreme effort to eject her from his room that night, even as he'd been physically *aching* to do something altogether different. It might have been legally acceptable, but it was still wrong in Myles' mind. She'd been too young besides being Rafe's sister. Neither argument had gone down well with Rae that night.

And all the while she'd been standing there in the flimsiest scraps of lace and his body had been under no illusions about how much he'd wanted her.

Even now, at the mere memory, his body tensed, coiled, like steel bands cinched tight on machinery, barely harnessing hundreds of pounds of pressure. The chemistry between him and Rae had been instantaneous. He'd tried to fight it, but it had been like nothing he'd ever experienced before. Its intensity had rocked him and it had only been the fact that she was his best friend's half-sister that had enabled Myles to walk away from her that last night when she'd offered herself to him completely. When she'd offered him the precious gift of her virginity.

That and the fact that he'd thought she deserved better than someone like him who might sleep with her once or twice and then would be gone. He'd thought *she* thought more of herself than to want someone like that.

And then she'd gone and not only thrown her virginity away on some wide boy like that bouncer, but she'd filmed it and leaked it to the press, as well.

Instantly he shut down the quiet doubt that had always nagged in the back of his mind.

Rafe had always claimed his half-sister had been innocent, but if that were true Rae herself would have told her side of it a long time ago.

He'd fallen for that innocent act once before. Surely he wasn't stupid enough to let himself be taken in by it a second time?

'I'm here because your brother asked for my help.' He injected a deliberately harder tone into his voice, reminding himself that nowadays he was immune to that look of hurt that skittered across her face. 'Not to blow smoke up each other's backsides.'

She blanched, but he had to admire the way she jutted her chin out that little bit more.

'I was merely complimenting a colleague. I had no idea it was so offensive to you.'

Her self-assurance was heady. He hadn't been prepared for quite how much of a woman Rae had grown into. But he could resist her, he'd proven it that night when the temptation had been immense.

So why, after all these years, did something still scrape away inside him making him feel raw and...*edgy*?

'I'm not here for you.' Was he repeating it for her benefit, or for his own? 'I'm here because Rafe asked me to be.'

'The same way you came to our home all those Christmases ago, because Rafe hadn't wanted to spend the holidays alone with his new stepfamily after his mother had just died?' she challenged.

'Rafe and I were recruits together. We did officers' training together.' Myles shrugged. 'They break down the individual and build up a team.'

'Is that why you tried to talk Rafe out of leaving when the stipulations in my father's will forced him to leave the British army and move to America to take over the Rawlstone Group instead?'

'Being an officer in the army was the one thing your old man knew Rafe truly loved. It was a power play from the grave.'

'Obviously.' She let out a humourless laugh. 'But why did you care so much?'

For a moment, Myles almost didn't answer.

'Because when I was on a medical mission that went south, Rafe's infantry unit was there. I owe my life to your brother.'

'Which is why you couldn't refuse his request to play at being my bodyguard.'

Something skittered over her features, too fast for him to read.

'Yes,' he bit out, instead.

He just hadn't banked on that old attraction roaring into life at the mere sound of her voice through a door. A chemistry like a volcano that had lain dormant for so long that it had fooled even himself into thinking it was extinct, but which now rumbled and heated and swelled within him.

And she was looking at him as though she felt exactly the same way.

'I'm glad it's you,' she whispered suddenly. 'I don't think I could have gone through with this if Rafe had found anyone else to play the part.'

Dammit, she was creeping under his skin and he didn't think she even knew it.

He couldn't allow her to know he still looked at her like that. That he still thought of her the way he had done fifteen years ago. That he still thought of her *at all*.

He tried reminding himself that his career as an army surgeon was all he'd ever needed.

But then he remembered that was gone, now—blown apart in an instant—and he had nothing.

Nothing to be proud of any more. Nothing to offer. Not to any woman, but certainly not to Rae. So, if he couldn't keep his tone even, controlled, neutral, then he was going to have to go the other way.

He was going to have to ensure that the last thing Rae wanted to do was revisit old haunts best left to rest.

'I owe Rafe. And if that means taking on the role of discreet bodyguard to his half-sister—' the words were deliberate, as if to wedge even more distance between them '—then I will. But believe me, Rae, as soon as it's over I'll be back out of your life faster than you can even turn around.'

* * *

Rae couldn't move, could barely even breathe, and she had no idea how she'd managed to answer him. Caught in a fist so tight that it felt as though it was crushing her soul right out of her chest.

She swallowed hard and plunged in.

'Fine. Then…we keep it strictly professional.'

'That would be best.'

He didn't blink, didn't even move. There was no trace at all that he even remembered the kisses they'd shared. The way he'd made her body come to life as no man ever had before.

Or since.

'Rafe mentioned that you've already completed the necessary qualifications and that you and he have been discussing a clinical observation role for some months already?'

'I'm weighing my options,' Myles confirmed curtly.

A coldness crept over her skin; the sense that he was trying to shut her out as much as possible. It shouldn't hurt. But it did.

She fought to peel her eyes off the man who stood, more imposing and mouth-watering than ever, in front of her. She failed.

He looked well.

Actually, he looked more than *well*. She wasn't sure when they'd closed the gap between them again, but he was so close now she had to tilt her head right up to maintain eye contact. To prove she wasn't really as intimidated as she felt. To pretend her heart wasn't doing odd...*flippy* things.

Myles was tall. She'd forgotten quite how tall. She wasn't exactly short to start with, but even wearing heels as she was, he still towered above her. Six feet three with shoulders wide enough to block out the view from even the expansive picture window behind him, but then a V-shaped chest tapered to a narrower waist, more athletic-fit than body-builder-fit, and powerful thighs encased in dark trousers. Familiar, and yet at the same time different.

His body itself looked like a weapon—precisely honed and utterly lethal, but it was more than that. He'd grown up, she realised with a start, and now he was more honed, more powerful, more...*dangerous*.

He positively exuded dominance, strength, control. As they stood there glowering at each other it was as though the last decade and a half toppled away without warning.

'I'm sorry.'

The apology was out before she even knew the words were on her tongue. But his scowl only deepened.

'What for?'

Rae hesitated. What *had* she meant? That night? Justin? Whatever had happened to Myles' distinguished army career?

Ultimately she shook her head, unable to articulate the thoughts that lurked in the fog of her mind, and the fringe that she'd been growing out, which was too long to be bangs but too short to tie back into her trademark ponytail, fell forward from behind her ear.

For a split second she thought his hand moved, as though about to tuck the hair back into place. And then she realised he was merely lifting his arms to fold across his chest, even as he took a step back. Putting more space between them, leaving her inexplicably bereft.

Had she imagined that instinctive, smouldering gaze from Myles? She must have, because the look he was casting her right now was, at best, one of distaste. At worst...

God, she still wanted him.

Realisation crashed over her like an icy wave on a scorching day. Because if she still wanted him, after everything, then she was as much in danger of making a fool of herself in front of the man as she had ever been.

And that simply couldn't happen.

Heat scorched her cheeks as Rae remembered the way she'd crept into Myles' room practically naked that last night and offered herself to him in the most intimate way she possibly could. He'd responded so urgently, so demandingly, so loaded with intent, she'd been lost in the moment and totally unprepared when he'd wrenched himself away, bundled her up into the quilt from the end of his guest suite bed, and pushed her unceremoniously back out into the corridor, slamming his bedroom door in her face.

He'd rejected her. Without a word of explanation. And she'd felt as though her world had crashed around her. The fact that he and Rafe had left the next day for some army exercise had meant that there had been no chance for her to get answers, and so for months she'd shut herself away wondering what was wrong with her. If she wasn't pretty enough, or sexy enough, or experienced enough.

Nonetheless, a bruised self-confidence didn't excuse the fact that she'd been stupid enough to fall for lies from a piece of trash like Justin. How had she ever thought that he could make her feel like an attractive woman again?

'You're sorry for what, Rae?' he repeated, his voice harsher than ever.

But if she couldn't explain it to herself, how could she explain it to Myles?

In all these years she'd never once explained herself to the press. Never once tried to put forward her side of that story. Not least because she knew no one would listen. Or if they did, they would spin it so that somehow she ended up coming out even worse.

Stupid, as well as scandalous.

More than that, if she'd told the truth, said that she'd known nothing about the camera, then it would have been a criminal offence and there would have had to have been a legal case.

Inevitably there would have been a character assassination of her, and even back then Rae had known that if the police and press had delved into her, then they might have found out about Myles.

She would have ruined his friendship with her half-brother, dragged his reputation through the mud, and even harmed his army career. All because she hadn't seen Justin for what he really was...a lying, scheming lowlife who just thought he could use her connection to *Life in the Rawl* to get his own fifteen minutes of fame.

Plus, she'd figured the less drama, the quicker it would all die down.

She'd been wrong. It had been too juicy for the press to let go of. It was only in the last few years of her becoming a fully-fledged doctor and OBGYN that they had finally begun to leave her alone and stop trying to connect her to any decent-looking male with a healthy pulse.

The silver lining, if she could call it that, was that she'd long since learned to *own* her mistakes. *Own* the woman those awful experiences had moulded her into. It had become her armour, her best emotional defence. And right now, with her head swirling wildly and thoughts jostling impatiently, she needed some way to buy herself time before she blurted everything out to him without first preparing the ground, and inevitably ruining her one opportunity to make him understand.

She needed something familiar. She needed some kind of anchor.

Even if a part of her knew that anchor was actually a tub of cement shoes ready to drown her at any moment.

She tipped her head almost coquettishly and

pulled her shoulders back in the kind of deliberately provocative move her sisters executed to devastating effect on practically a daily basis, but which she hadn't used in years.

'Forget it.' She even managed to force the beginnings of a wicked little smile, even if her cheeks did feel tight and unwilling. 'I wasn't really thinking.'

Myles locked his jaw and she could practically see the tiny pulse flickering away.

'Of course not,' he ground out. 'Because why change the habit of a lifetime?'

'Why indeed?'

She didn't care that he was staring at her as though she were a fleck of contemptible mud on the toe of one of his polished army boots. Really she didn't.

Not, she imagined, that he would *ever* tolerate any form of dirt on his parade boots.

And it didn't twist inside her to know that he, like pretty much the rest of the world, actually believed that she had ever had any part in that vile sex tape. There was no reason for this shameful heat that spread over her cheeks. She'd long since mastered the art of pretending that it didn't get to her. If she could fool the press, the public, then she could certainly fool Myles.

Tilting her head that little bit higher, Rae forced herself—however many knives stabbed into the dark hollow where her soul had once been—to meet his glower.

As if she were simply playing the game he evidently thought she was playing, although her voice damn near cracked when she answered him.

Myles narrowed his eyes but she ignored it.

'Well, now we have those *pleasantries* out of the way—' she rolled her eyes to make her point '—I think it's time for me to go. I have a lecture to get ready for. Doctor or not, I find the press prefer glamorous photos to dowdy shots.'

'Is that so?' Myles pursed his lips and she knew he was thinking of the sex tape.

Just as she'd intended, she told herself.

It was the only way.

Other than Rafe, Myles was the only other man alive who she'd ever wanted to impress. She couldn't explain it, but in some perverse way she would prefer he hated her for the choices he thought she *had* made, than know she was so pathetic that she'd let someone like Justin play her.

She scowled at him, and in that moment something crossed his face, pulling his features and making her look again.

She realised abruptly that he didn't look as well as she'd initially thought. Or, more accurately, he looked physically incredible, but *non-physically...*?

Her heart kicked before she could stop it and it was all she could do not to reach out and touch his tense, strained face. His eyes were darker than she remembered. Bleaker. Grim and laced with pain.

Her head swam with echoes of her half-brother's words outside the doors just before they'd entered the room. That Myles needed their help.

She had known that Myles had spent most of his career as a battlefield trauma surgeon with a specialty in plastic surgery—specifically with burns from bombs, IEDs and mines. But hearing that Myles had been caught up in it, injured so badly that he'd chosen to leave the army altogether rather than fly a desk, was sickening.

It had been awful hearing Rafe tell her that Myles, having been authorised to return to operating, had turned down lucrative job offers with hospitals up and down the UK, as well as opportunities in multiple top US hospitals.

It had taken her a while to understand what Rafe had been suggesting.

'I think that right now Myles needs to see

other specialties of medicine.' Rafe's caginess
had snagged her attention. 'I need you to help
him, Rae.'

It was the closest she'd ever heard her half-
brother get to a plea.

'Let him see a different side to being a surgeon. One which doesn't involve suicide bomb-
ers, and maimed kids, and putting your closest
buddies in a body bag.'

She'd felt sick on Myles' behalf.

She could have told her brother that being an
OBGYN wasn't all hearts and flowers; that death
touched this area of medicine, too. But somehow
it didn't seem the same. Especially when she remembered the look on Rafe's face when he'd told
her that a lance corporal, a mere kid, had taken
his own life that day, and that he feared Myles
blamed himself.

'Is he right to?' Rae had asked abruptly.

She hadn't meant to, but she'd suddenly found
that she was shaking and this was the only way
she could stop it.

'Of course not.' Rafe had looked momentarily
annoyed, before making a clear effort to soften
his tone. 'Please, Rae? You'd be solving two
problems for me. You would be getting a bodyguard we can both trust. And you would poten-

tially be helping the man who showed me how to be the best leader and soldier I could possibly be.'

The pain on his face had got to her. But it was nothing like the expression she was looking at right now on Myles' face. Fifteen years ago she would have ached to steal that pain away for him. *But not now*, she told herself firmly. *Not now.*

Rae wasn't sure she believed herself or why the words sounded so hollow in her head.

But still, she would do what Rafe had asked her to do. Not just because it was her half-brother asking, but because, deep down, they both knew she liked to fix people. She couldn't fix her own life so she concentrated on others'. It was probably one of the reasons why being an OBGYN suited her so well. There were always dark moments but in this field the outcome was more often positive, especially when it entailed bringing a new life into the world, and into the arms of an ecstatic mother.

If that couldn't shine some light into whatever dark pit Myles was in, then surely nothing could?

And the fact that she was the one helping him—that maybe she could prove to him she was a skilled, professional OBGYN and that the incident with Justin, for which she'd become infamous, was nothing more than a brief, shameful moment in her past—had nothing to do with it.

'You know you can talk to me, Myles,' she began impulsively. 'I'm a good listener...whatever you're going through.'

She knew immediately it had been the wrong thing to say.

'Did you manage to sleep on the flight?' he asked abruptly.

How she wished she could take her words back. Swallow them. Instead, she tried to regulate her breathing enough to answer.

'Yes.'

Seven hours of blissful, uninterrupted sleep in the company jet's bedroom suite had inarguably been more comfortable than the doctor's accommodation at the New York clinic where she'd snatched the odd hour or so whilst pulling her second thirty-six-hour shift of the week.

'Clearly it wasn't enough—you still look tired.' He peered at her, concerned.

It was hard to ooze the nonchalance for which she was so ironically well known when her whole body was going into overdrive at the mere suggestion of solicitude from him.

'Gosh, thanks for the compliment.'

She even managed to keep her voice from shaking, but Myles ignored her dry tone.

'You should look after yourself more.' He apparently felt the need to hammer home the point.

Rae chastised herself for hoping for something more praiseworthy from him.

'Says the man who, if you're anything like my brother, exists on four hours' sleep a night.' She kept her laugh deliberately light.

He shrugged as though it was okay for him.

Her chest cracked.

So much for Myles being her bodyguard, meant to protect her, to ensure she didn't get hurt. As far as Rae was concerned, he was the one person who could wound her more deeply than anyone else ever could.

Just as he had done before.

Clearly fifteen years had taught her absolutely nothing.

CHAPTER THREE

'CASE C CONCERNS emergency foetal intervention at twenty-five weeks and four days into the pregnancy, for a sacrococcygeal teratoma. That is, a congenital tumour growing at the base of the foetus' spine. It is one of the most common tumours amongst neonatals, occurring in approximately one in every forty thousand babies. But because it arises from stem cells it can be made up of any kind of tissue from anywhere around the body.'

It took a while for Myles to realise that he was as caught up in her lecture, her enthusiasm for her subject matter, as everyone else in the ballroom.

She looked magnificent up there on the stage and holding the entire conference in silent rapture. He had hugely underestimated her. Underestimated the residual feelings that still ran between them, and now he was here. Paying the price.

He tuned back in, unable to help himself.

'Ultrasound. And because the teratoma has a blood supply, the baby's heart was pumping much harder. It was as if they were in competition and the tumour was winning, resulting in a significant risk of the baby going into cardiac arrest.'

Myles shifted his position.

He'd been a battlefield trauma surgeon for so long. He'd never imagined doing anything else. Never wanted to.

But that was before.

In seventeen years, nothing had quite got to him like that day with Mikey, and what had happened in that village. And, suddenly, he'd found himself never wanting to pick up another scalpel for the rest of his life. Not because he was afraid of what he might do. But more he was afraid of what he might no longer be able to do.

Ever.

PTSD. Not uncommon after so many back-to-back tours, and so many atrocities, but that didn't make it any easier to accept. It didn't make the idea of going back to operating any more appealing. Which was why accepting Rafe's suggestion of clinical observation—a sort of halfway house—had made sense, even if he hadn't actually *liked* the idea.

He had his qualifications. And it wasn't as though he was doing anything else. The death threats to Rafe's family had been the proverbial added bonus. The tie-in with Rae almost like fate. He focussed back on Rae.

'The de-bulking of the tumour on the actual foetus usually takes less than half an hour,' she was telling them. 'The majority of the five-hour operation is spent opening up the uterus in the first instance, and then stitching it closed again. Our biggest concern is to avoid compromising the health of the mother, and we have to make sure the uterus is sealed and watertight.'

Fascinated, he allowed himself to be absorbed by her presentation. Her care for her patients shone through her excitement for the skilled procedure. She handled the questions well, informing without patronising, always happy to elaborate or explain.

For a moment, Myles forgot everything. Who he was. Where. Why. And just let his old enthusiasm for medicine begin to slowly unfurl. Then the ballroom erupted into applause, and Myles made his way backstage to meet her.

It hit him even before he turned around. The

shift in the atmosphere, the way the air seemed to close in on him. When he turned around, she almost stole the breath from his lungs.

It wasn't Rae's looks that struck him, although she was certainly attractive. She'd always been attractive, and that hadn't changed. But this was something more. A presence, an aura, for want of a better term. She carried herself better than she once had, but with none of the arrogant hauteur he'd been expecting.

Unsettled, he could only stare in silence for what was a split second but felt more like a minute; fighting the sensation that he was actually drowning in his own lungs.

When had they closed the gap between the two of them? And why did the unexpected proximity send a slew of memories cascading through his brain, all of which centred on the chemistry that had arced between them that Christmas, the hot glances and the bodies brushing against each other in the long corridors of that old house?

And now those shrewd eyes were assessing him. Judging *him*.

'Good lecture. I'm glad to see that you've finally found something for which it's worth being well known.'

It was a low, cruel blow, and he loathed himself for it. As though he was deliberately trying to goad her. To remind her of the girl who had leaked a sex tape, which Rafe had only found out about when some of his men had been watching it online, in the middle of a tour of duty.

To remind her of the girl who had offered him her virginity first.

What was he angrier about? That she hadn't waited for him? Or that she'd rubbed his face in it by doing it for a sex tape for the world to see?

Or maybe he was trying to remind *himself* of that girl, since his body appeared to be reacting to her in a way of which his brain unquestionably disapproved.

She blinked, a faint stain spreading across her cheeks, and if he hadn't known it to be impossible he'd have thought he saw a flash of shame and regret in those forest depths. But then it was gone and she eyed him with distaste.

'Which is fortunate for you, since you're to be shadowing me.'

He tried to pretend her voice didn't tremble a little at the end. That she was still as strong as she was clearly pretending to be. Because otherwise it might make him soften all the more towards her.

And that wouldn't be acceptable. There was

clearly more wrong with his state of mind than he had feared.

Then she crossed her arms over her chest as if it could somehow provide her with some degree of armour, when all it really did was highlight the generous breasts Myles was unexpectedly having to fight to pretend he didn't notice.

Lust barrelled through him. As shocking and unwelcome as it was unstoppable. Making his body fire up like a mark five thunder flash.

In some perverse way, he almost welcomed it. Ever since that last mission he'd been numb. Unable to feel, to want, anything. In the six months since he'd left the army he'd been existing, not living.

At least this—whatever *this* was—made a change from the hollow, empty *nothingness* that had swirled around his chest for so long now, like the dark waters moving perniciously beneath the blue marble of an ice road, ready to claim a life the moment that sheet barrier grew too thin. Ready to erupt in a blowout at the first opportunity.

It was time to open the memories on the girl he'd once known. To finally acknowledge that he might have been mistaken in what he'd thought about her all these years.

Almost against his better judgement, he found himself employing one of the skills he'd perfected so well throughout his career.

The ability to re-evaluate.

Her hair, as long, thick, and glossy brown as he remembered, was pulled back into an attractive yet practical ponytail thing. Her clothes were professional yet subtly sexy and she wore no false nails, or eyelashes, or caked-on make-up. In fact, he couldn't be sure she was wearing any make-up at all, her face was so clear, so soft.

Horrified, he realised his fingers were actually itching to touch her, to see if she was as smooth as she looked. He balled them quickly and resisted the urge to shove them in his pockets. Yet her eyes flickered, as though she somehow knew.

His head was already a mess without the complication of attraction. He felt like that angry, desperate twenty-one-year-old all over again, not knowing where his life was heading but knowing he needed to take the only chance he had to get away from the nightmare childhood that had made nasty Ronald Rawlstone look like Father of the Year.

That Christmas with Rae had been the only

time he'd ever stopped, and wondered, and wanted. Even if she'd never known it.

He needed to understand if he really had been a gullible idiot to have lain there that night and wondered if he should just walk out of his room, down that hallway, and risk it all to be with her.

'I was with Rafe on his last tour of duty when your father died. When you leaked that ignominious sex tape,' he said quietly. 'I was with him when we walked in on men, soldiers under his command, watching you…frolic…on-screen.'

She blanched but he forced himself to go on. Pretending it hadn't seared him as much as it had seared Rafe, if for very different reasons. Pretending he hadn't harboured secret fantasies of returning to the US after his tour of duty and making good on the offer she'd presented him with on that crazy night.

If he pretended it was just about the way she'd let down Rafe, and not about his own hurt pride, then maybe it could be true.

'Your brother…half-brother, had to command those men. Up until that moment, he'd been respected by those men. After that, things changed.'

'I didn't…' She faltered, then stopped.

'You didn't what?' Myles echoed.

But she didn't answer. She simply shook her head.

And what galled him the most was that suddenly there was a small, hitherto non-existent part of him that desperately wanted to hear her say something, anything, to make it less unpalatable.

It made absolutely no sense. And yet he *ached*.

They were standing close. Too close. He could feel her breath on his chest, rapid and shallow. The temptation to step forward, to lift his hands to her face, to...what? *Kiss her?* That couldn't happen.

He had no idea how he managed it, but, abruptly, he took a step backwards. Was the distance a blessing or a curse?

Rae stood motionless, silently willing Myles to stop moving away from her, though she couldn't explain why.

Her eyes were still locked with his, which were the same intense colour as the most turquoise-blue waters that lapped at her favourite Caribbean island. Eyes that had plagued her darkest dreams for the last decade. He might as well have weaved some kind of spell over her at that first encounter all those years ago.

But, more than that, she'd seen the respect when he and her brother had approached each other, she'd heard the fondness, and suddenly she found herself craving it, too.

To be on the receiving end of a warm look from Major Myles Garrington, instead of a look that suggested he considered her on a par with the dirt on the sole of his shoe.

He'd changed so much in the last fifteen years. He was now so solid, so unyielding, so authoritative. And yet, in some way she couldn't put her finger on, he hadn't changed a bit.

It left her feeling strangely rattled. Undone.

'You didn't what?' Myles pressed again.

She wanted to tell him that she wasn't the woman the press made her out to be. That the only man she'd ever been intimate with had been Justin. That she'd thought herself in love. That he'd assured her *he* had been in love.

She could almost taste the words on her tongue, sweet syllables that could free her.

Or condemn her.

Because she knew what her reputation with the salivating press was. Knew what the public thought of her. And even if none of that were true, hadn't she thrown herself at Myles that New Year's Eve? Of course he was going to believe she was capable of doing exactly the same thing with Justin only months later.

He would never believe that wasn't at all how it had happened that night.

The best thing she could do would be to forget any history with Myles. But surely it was impossible *not* to notice the man now looming in front of her? The man who had always been *good-looking* but who now made that term seem flimsy and two-dimensional.

His handsome qualities had long since segued into something more brooding, more weathered. His strong features now had character. They told a story. She was already spellbound, and it frightened her. Just like the lines etched softly onto his skin, which suggested he'd been places, seen things, *done* things. He was a hard, autocratic, lethal kind of handsome.

'I didn't *frolic*,' she bit out abruptly.

His mouth curled ever so slightly, his antipathy surely evident. Yet inexplicably it only made her traitorous fingers twitch to reach out and touch those unusually bow-shaped lips; the dimple gave him the most glorious cleft chin.

Would it still feel the same as it once did beneath her fingertips?

Before, when she'd said she'd been *expecting someone...more*, it struck her that what she'd really meant was someone *less*. Someone who didn't affect her anywhere near the way this one man affected her. Someone who didn't make her feel as though she were searing from the inside out. Cauterised by his every mocking look, desiccating from his indifferent tone.

Just as she always had been.

'Of course not,' he replied silkily. 'Because you're the steadfast, quiet Rawlstone sister, with no press reputation at all. Forgive me but I forgot.'

She flashed her brightest smile.

The one that she had long ago learned best concealed all the hurt inside her.

She knew exactly what the press said about her, every line, every lie. Which made it a hard reputation to shake. Although, by God, she'd tried.

But whilst Rafe might appreciate how she'd struggled to distance herself from her mother and sisters all this time, the press weren't always as understanding; the public not completely forgiving.

Neither was Myles, standing there, judging her

as he was. She felt weighed and she felt measured, but what bothered her more was the shame flooding through her body at the realisation that this man...*this* man...found her deplorably wanting.

How was it that his opinion of her mattered so much more than that of hundreds, even thousands, of other people? The way he'd got under her skin with barely a word was shocking. Frightening. Not least because of last time. What was the matter with her? She wrinkled her nose in self-castigation, blurting words out before her brain had the chance to engage.

'Why are you doing this, Myles? Just so you can taunt me?' Her pitch was rising but she couldn't seem to control it. 'Just so you can remind me of the fool I made of myself when I crept into your room practically naked, stupidly—so stupidly—imagining that the kiss we'd shared earlier that evening meant you wanted me?'

'This isn't about that night,' he rasped, his voice so unrecognisable that it took a moment for her to realise it really was him.

'It isn't?' she whispered.

'No, Raevenne, it's definitely *not* about that night.' There was no mistaking the look of utter disgust that contorted his features now.

She tried to rearm herself but it was too late, and his loathing smashed over her with deadly force.

'I try not to remember that night. It isn't difficult. It isn't something I ever care to think about. I thought you were different, Rae, I thought you were someone else, someone worth being honourable for.'

'Yeah, well, having a door slammed in my face certainly didn't feel *honourable*.'

She didn't know why she was fighting back. What she was hoping to achieve.

'You offered me your virginity.'

'I know what I did.' Her whole body felt as though it were on fire. 'And I know you practically laughed me out your room.'

'I believed I was doing the right thing. I thought…' He paused as if having to catch himself. 'I thought your innocence meant more to you than it obviously did. I was leaving, as soon as that Christmas break was up and Rafe felt as though he'd done his duty. I felt you deserved more than someone who slept with you once or twice and then cut out, never to be seen again.'

'It did mean something to me—' she began.

A brash, humourless laugh, which she barely even recognised, cut her off.

'Of course it did. So much so, in fact, that you not only slept with the next guy you dated- and I use that term very loosely- but you filmed the whole thing and leaked it on the Internet all in the name of fame.'

Nausea crashed over her and it was all she could do to fight it back. Still, she couldn't stop herself from crying out.

'I didn't know anything about it. I didn't know he was filming me. I certainly didn't leak it. My God, is that really how little you think of me?'

'That's bull,' Myles growled, ignoring her question. 'If you hadn't known anything about it then he would have been filming a sex act without consent. That's a criminal offence. You would have said something. He would have been convicted. He *should* have been convicted. But instead you stayed quiet. You protected him. Why do that unless you were in on it, too?'

She wanted to tell him. She'd imagined this moment so very many times over the years. But the words wouldn't come. Something seemed to be stopping her.

'I was pathetic, naïve, desperate and I didn't want to look any more of an idiot than I already did.' The words tumbled out inelegantly.

The harsh bark was about as far from a laugh as it was possible to get.

'Oh, come on, Rae. You can't seriously expect *anyone* to believe that. You weren't protecting yourself, you were protecting *him*.'

She shook her head, hating the very idea of that.

'I wasn't. I never protected him. I hate him. I…' She bit her lip and then decided she had nothing left to lose. 'I was protecting you.'

The silence that descended on them was so instant, so heavy, that for a moment she thought her eardrums had burst and all she could sense was a ringing in her head. For long, long moments they stood, eyes locked, perfectly still, and then Myles spoke.

'Say again?' Dark, forbidding. It wasn't exactly the response she'd been hoping for.

Rae drew in a deep breath, her voice quaking unrecognisably.

'I was protecting *you*,' she practically whispered. 'Just like you protected me that night when we were kids. You were so principled even though you were only three years older than me. Telling me I was too innocent, too young emotionally, that I might hate myself when you left, that I was Rafe's sister.'

Not that it had made her feel any better, and less *rejected*, at the time. Even now she couldn't shake the knowledge that if she'd been sexy and worldly like her sisters, even at seventeen, he couldn't have walked away from her however principled he was.

But that was a truth she would always hug to herself. A truth too embarrassing to voice aloud to anyone. Ever.

He didn't answer, but the locked jaw told her that he was barely containing his fury. She hurried on before he could say any words she didn't want to hear.

'If I *had* told people that I hadn't consented then there would have had to have been an investigation. It would have been my word against his. They would have looked at my sexual history. And they might have found out about you.'

'We didn't do anything,' Myles growled, his obvious contempt slicing through her more deeply than she could have thought imaginable.

In all her scenarios over the years, she'd never once considered that he wouldn't believe her. How foolish that seemed now.

'But *they* might not have believed we didn't do anything,' she cried. 'And you know what they say about mud sticking. Your name would have been dragged into it whether we liked it or not. The press would have loved any whiff of scandal concerning a supposedly principled British army officer. The truth wouldn't have mattered. Your reputation would have been tainted for ever.'

'You really want me to believe you let people think and say everything they did about you to protect me?'

Disgust, and what looked terrifyingly like hatred, clouded his face. It was all Rae could do not to shrink away, even as something tore at her heart.

'It's the truth.' She had no idea how she held her ground. 'But it wasn't just about you. Like I said, it was about me, too. Whatever I said wouldn't have undone what had happened. That video would always be out there...*will* always be out there. And there would have been no guarantee they'd have believed me over Justin. So I tried to make the best out of it. I figured it would die down when the next scandal came along.'

She could never have imagined what a miscalculation that would be.

Probably about as gigantic a blunder as blurting out the truth now and allowing herself to think, even for a moment, that Myles would believe her.

Even forgive her.

Instead she found herself staring into the glacial depths.

'Myles—'

'I don't want to hear any more.' He cut her pleading off abruptly.

'I really—'

'I said *enough*, Raevenne.'

She bit her tongue. She could refuse to be cowed by him but what good would it do to force the issue? It would only make him shut down all the more.

If that was even possible.

So instead she stood still, too afraid even to shift her weight from one foot to the other, as if they were teetering on the edge of some abyss and the slightest movement could send them plummeting down.

She wasn't even sure if she remembered to keep breathing.

And then, finally, Myles spoke.

'This was a mistake.'

She opened her mouth to reply but he silenced her again.

'You don't want a bodyguard and I sure as hell don't want to play one.'

Somehow, incredibly, given the maelstrom raging inside her chest, she stayed standing. Stayed...impassive.

'I'll tell Rafe this isn't going to work.'

She should be pleased. Relieved. Wasn't this what she'd told her half-brother less than twelve hours ago? That she didn't want a bodyguard again, reminding the press of her past.

So why was a part of her silently screaming out to Myles not to do this?

'I thought you said you owed him.' She had no idea how she kept her voice from breaking.

'I'll find some other way to repay him,' Myles bit out.

She opened her mouth, then closed it again.

She had no idea how long they stood there after that. It felt like a lifetime but it was probably no more than thirty seconds. Until the shrill sound of a mobile cut through the air, making Rae jump.

Was it her imagination or did Myles hesitate for a fraction of a moment before answering it?

'Garrington.' As his eyes lifted back to hers, his expression utterly impassive, something Rae couldn't identify snaked through her. 'When?

How? Understood. Follow the SOPs, keep me apprised.'

He terminated the call, his focus still locked onto Rae. She ran a tongue over suddenly inexplicably dry lips.

'What is it?'

'Change of plan.' His voice still gave nothing away, although for a brief moment something skittered across his features before it was gone. If she hadn't known better she might have thought it was concern. 'I'll be your bodyguard for the foreseeable.'

She tried to control the panic rising inside her.

'What's going on, Myles?'

He paused for a moment before dipping his head in a ghost of a nod.

'Your Manhattan home has been broken into. There's a fair amount of damage.'

She was going to be sick.

'Opportunists?' she managed to get out.

'At this point I don't know. It could be coincidence, but I can't rule out the possibility that it's related to these death threats.'

'Myles—'

'Rafe has the company jet ready. You'll need to get home to confirm as soon as possible if anything is missing so we have a better idea if it was a directed attack.'

'I can't.' She shook her head frantically. 'I can't do this alone.'

Vaguely, she was aware of Myles taking her hand.

'You won't be alone, Rae.' His voice sounded gritty, lower, but her head was spinning too much to be sure. 'I'm not going anywhere. I won't let anything happen to you.'

And with that he erased the confrontation of the last twelve hours as if it had never existed.

The tears came without warning, silent and hot, but suddenly she was stepping towards him, a part of her desperately needing his warmth and strength. And then his arms were around her and she was drawing comfort from him.

'I can't stay in the house,' she muttered against the solid wall of his chest.

'We'll go to a hotel. I won't leave your side.'

'Promise me?'

He paused, and when he spoke again his grave voice rumbled deep inside her.

'I promise, Rae.'

Later, much later, when she was alone in the company jet bedroom, she would remember that moment. The way he hadn't exactly enfolded her in his arms willingly, but he hadn't exactly pushed her away, either.

She would wonder at the sanity of staying in a hotel with him whilst her emotions seemed to be so scattered, so fluttery, and she would conclude that sleeping in the hospital's on-call rooms would be infinitely safer, both mentally and physically.

And yet she would wonder if, after all, she might finally be able to convince him that she wasn't the woman the world all too often made her out to be, but more like the girl he remembered from that Christmas all those years ago.

CHAPTER FOUR

'COME ON. EMERGENCY C-SECTION.' Rae spoke crisply as she hurried down the stairs to the operating rooms, taking the steps two at a time.

They'd barely spoken since that night she'd given the lecture back in the UK. The night when he'd come so close to letting her see just how easily she could wrap him around her little finger. Still.

The night he'd hit back the only way he'd known how, but which had given him no pleasure and had, if anything, made him feel like a complete bastard. Since then, he'd accompanied her to her home to check what had been stolen, all of which had confirmed his suspicion that the break-in wasn't opportunists but was somehow connected to the death threats.

He'd stayed with her at the hospital whilst a team cleared up her home, but otherwise they'd only conversed on a medical basis.

He should be pleased. He should feel victorious. They had sidestepped the inappropriate attraction that, as ludicrous as it was, lurked between them even after all these years, and put things on a purely professional footing.

Instead he felt oddly deflated. Oddly...at sea.

It wasn't just concern for her personal safety and the knowledge that Rafe's fears weren't entirely unfounded. Although he had to admit, both of these facts had affected him far more than they had any business doing.

It felt somehow more personal than it should do.

'Veronica is a thirty-six-year-old parturient,' Rae hurried on, forcing him to pull his head back into the game. 'She arrived on the labour ward a few hours ago, five centimetres dilated and progressing nicely. However, she's subsequently developed heavy bleeding and the baby's heart rate began to drop dangerously low. Suspected placental abruption, which an ultrasound has appeared to confirm.'

He might have been an army surgeon for his whole career, but he could remember back to his training enough to know that when the placenta detached from the uterus wall prematurely, it could be life-threatening for the baby, who could be deprived of nutrients and oxygen. Not to mention the bleeding. But Rae had said the baby still had a heart rate.

'Partial abruption?' he verified.

'Yes, but it could turn severe at any time, which is why we're going in for the baby.'

'Understood.'

Dr Raevenne Rawlstone, his mind wandered again as they moved swiftly through the corridor.

She wasn't at all what he'd been expecting and, as galling as it was to admit it, over these last couple of days, she'd thrown him. Perhaps even more than she had back in the UK less than a week ago.

And it had been one thing reading about her success and skill as a doctor from afar, but it was quite another experiencing it first-hand. She was also a surprisingly generous teacher.

And he could only admire the fact that she'd pushed some society gala—due to start in an hour—in order to extend her thirty-six-hour shift into something even more inhuman.

She was more like the army surgeons he'd worked with, shoulder to shoulder, for so many years, and it was beginning to make him...*home-sick*? Homesick for operating.

It was entirely unsettling.

And that was without the added complication

that he'd been pretending hadn't existed ever since that first meeting in Rafe's offices, of that ridiculous attraction that still smouldered between them.

Wholly incongruous and utterly inappropriate.

Yet, there it was. Still sizzling in every unguarded look, hastily smothered into a deep scowl, every careless brush against the other, which was instantly replaced by a deliberate step away, every time they came to the same medical conclusion only for the moment of connection to be immediately severed by some imaginary scalpel.

He could recall with all too startling clarity the occasion her hair had grazed his forearm at some point when they'd been examining the same chart, and a jolt of electricity had snaked its way up his biceps, across his shoulder and right through his chest. Or the deep shiver that had run through Rae's body when she'd reached across him for the ultrasound machine and his breath had lifted the hairs slightly on the back of her neck.

She'd lingered just that fraction too long and he, foolishly, hadn't been able to help himself repeating the action.

He caught himself shortly after that; tried to

remind himself of exactly who Raevenne was, and precisely why Rafe had employed him.

These moments of weakness wouldn't be happening again. He refused to let them.

'Which is why we need to deliver the baby by C-section before the abruption is complete.' Rae shouldered the door open as they hurried to scrub in. 'I'm guessing you didn't do many C-sections in your time as an army trauma surgeon?'

'It wasn't really a common procedure, no,' he demurred. 'Although I have assisted in a couple. All of the field hospitals I worked in treated civilians as well as allied and enemy soldiers, although usually for injuries. But some of the civilians were pregnant women and sometimes the injury meant the baby was coming out whether we liked it or not.'

'Okay, well, now you get to see it day in and day out. Then it's up to you to decide whether changing speciality to OBGYN is for you.'

Something unexpectedly hot wound through him at her clipped tone.

How much of his recent events did she know?

Tucking the question to the back of his mind, Myles scrubbed up and followed her into her operating room. He knew that, even after this, she still wouldn't go to the ball until she'd checked on her last patient, the seven-months-pregnant woman who had been admitted with significant bleeding after falling off a ladder while trying to decorate a Christmas tree for her three-year-old daughter.

Exquisite.

Her fitted dress showcased every delectable curve to perfection without being too revealing, her dark hair swept off her neck and piled artfully on her head like the rich, chocolate mirror coating of the dessert he already knew was her favourite indulgence after a long, gruelling shift.

It was only one of a multitude of insignificant facts he should not have taken the time to learn about her at all. He'd told himself that moving into her house with her was a sensible precaution after the break-in. That it was his job, that Rafe was paying him to be as vigilant with his sister as they'd always been *out there*.

Deep down he suspected there was something far less noble—and something far more primal—behind his decision.

He had never understood Rafe's misplaced sense of protectiveness towards Rae after the tape had come out. Yet now, here he was, watching Rae circulate the ballroom, with something reeling and circling his chest that he feared was all too close to that same protectiveness.

Her passion for the charity shone out of her like a glorious, golden light, buoying the guests and instilling them with the pre-Christmas spirit on what was otherwise a dreary November night.

A night which was all about raising enough money to buy Christmas gifts for displaced and refugee children, and ship them worldwide in time for the special celebrations.

Though why Rae needed anyone else to help her was beyond him—surely her enthusiasm alone could have filled up this ballroom ten times over.

She was charming guest after guest as though she didn't know that they would delight in making vicious, cruel comments behind her back as soon as she'd left. He watched them do it.

Could practically hear their ugly, bitter laughter from across the room.

His hands clenched in the pockets of his tuxedo. Forget two-faced, most of these people were more like forty-faced. They didn't deserve so much as the time of day from a woman who had, up until an hour ago, been delivering triplets in the most complicated birth he'd seen to date.

There were women here he could well imagine had been primping and preening all day, at least, just *to be seen* at this supposedly philanthropic event. Rae, however, had shucked off her operating garb, dashed in and out of the shower and dried her hair courtesy of a quick blast crouched under the hand-dryers, and had been in the car ten minutes later applying her make-up and dictating medical notes.

Yet she eclipsed every single person in the room.

She shimmered amongst them, delicate and breathtaking. Like the most glorious butterfly flitting amongst a deadly cluster of predatory dragonflies.

The army had honed his observation skills to perfection over the years, yet it had felt as fascinating, as *game changing*, as it did right now. He took in everything, his mind processing it and trying to make sense of it all. From the close-knit team back in the hospital who, to his surprise, clearly adored their hard-working Dr Rawlstone, to the guests who barely retracted their claws as they fawned over Rae at this ball.

Only one thing stopped them from being rude to Rae's face. They might feed off her long-time bad-girl reputation, but she was still a Rawlstone and these people knew the value of that. Which was why they laughed and fawned over her, and pledged hundreds, thousands, even tens of thousands in some cases, of dollars to the charity that Rae so earnestly promoted.

And all those vainglorious men, who laughed so uproariously when their jealous partners sniped about Rae, all the while not so secretly coveting her. Men who took every excuse to touch her, who undressed her with their eyes, who would sleep with her in a heartbeat only to, he was sure, turn around and plead they had been involuntarily seduced by her.

There was no reason whatsoever for him to feel aggrieved on Rae's behalf.

Certainly not for the shards of possessiveness that lanced through him when he was least expecting them. The way his hands itched to run over her unequivocally sexy, feminine form. Or the way he felt altogether too hot, too wired, too greedy, as he struggled to drag his eyes from the way she sashayed around the floor.

But he didn't try too hard. Myles reminded himself that it was his job to watch her, to ensure she was safe. It was what Rafe had brought him in to do. He firmly quashed any other thoughts in his head.

Abruptly Rae stiffened, her expression becoming that little bit frozen, her movements less fluid. He followed her line of sight, ready to move, although he knew from the silence in his earpiece that she was in no physical danger.

It wasn't hard to spot what had unsettled her.

Her sisters were making their way towards Rae, along with the matriarch of the Rawlstone Rabble, their tight expressions and false smiles evident even from this distance. From the way they were bearing down on her, they weren't intending to merely compliment her on a successful charity gala. Or at least, any compliments would most certainly be like roses. Beautiful on the surface but with well-placed barbs designed to draw blood if one was foolish enough to forget to look out for them.

He started forward, only to stop himself. Rae's family was *her* problem. He was here to protect her from any maniac stalker, he wasn't here to protect her from her *tiger shark* relatives. If her sisters ganged up to feast on the weaker one, then surely that was for Rae to deal with herself. Wasn't he forgetting that at one time they'd all been as bad as each other?

Yet since when had he thought her the vulnerable one? Only a week ago he'd thought of her as a highly skilled predator herself.

What was the matter with him?

And then she looked up, her gaze snagging his, the frantic glimmer in her eyes tugging at him even across the vast ballroom. He knew it wasn't his situation to resolve—he should stand his ground, continue observing the guests. But suddenly he was moving again, parting the buzzing throngs with the same ease with which he had parted villagers in the crowded towns when on patrol. Gaps opened up for him and closed behind him without him having to say a word, without him even having to look twice, so that before he had time to talk himself out of it he was there.

Standing next to her. Pretending his body hadn't just gone up in flames the second her arm had slipped around his in a grip that was too tight to even attempt to conceal her anxiety; the second she'd edged closer to him as though she thought he was some kind of protector.

'Who would have thought that you would object so vociferously to a bodyguard when your life might be in danger from a stranger,' he murmured darkly, 'yet leap at the chance to have one when you're in the sights of mere family.'

'Given that you've done little to hide your opinion that my side of the Rawlstone family is trashy, I can't imagine you're really all that surprised.'

Her response might have been pitched only for his ears, but its unexpected feistiness rippled through him. Something he might have mistaken for *pride*, if he hadn't known better, swirled around the two of them.

'Clearly I was mistaken in thinking your look from across this immense room was a plea for help. You can obviously look after yourself.'

Her grip tightened on him.

'Of course I can, I've been doing it long enough. But, since you're here, you might as well stay.'

A week ago he might not have recognised the faintest of tremors in her tone. What did it say that he recognised it, now? That it made him nudge that little bit further forward with his body, as though to shield her that fraction better?

And then her family were there, and her grip on him loosened only long enough to accept their greeting.

'I hope you're working the room properly, *pug*.' The fake air kisses set his teeth on edge almost as much as the deliberate slur. 'This is quite an event we're championing here tonight.'

Pug. How had he forgotten the cruel nickname her sisters had given her? Because she'd followed him around that Christmas holiday just like their neighbour's ugly old pug.

'I expect it to be a massive success if I'm putting my name to it,' another sniffed.

As if it were *their* victory rather than Rae's, Myles thought. As if they'd done more than simply show up having been made-up and coiffured to within an inch of their inconsequential lives.

'It's already a success,' Rae tried to assert.

'Front-page-news success?' Her mother arched one condescending eyebrow. 'I don't think so. You need to do better, Raevenne.'

'I am—'

'Six-figure sums, child,' the older woman snapped.

'That only happens when someone gets the ball rolling. Like the Jenning family. And, after all, Mariella Jenning is one of your best friends, Mother.'

'I lunch with that woman.' The feigned shudder was purely for dramatic effect. 'You can't possibly ask me to stoop so low as to ask her for money.'

'For charity,' Rae cried before appearing to catch herself as her sisters laughed scornfully.

'Don't be absurd, *pug*.'

'Fine, well, how about Rowena Kemp? You don't lunch with her.'

'Are you insane? You expect the first time I speak to a member of the illustrious Kemp family to be asking for handouts?'

'Donations.' Rae gritted her teeth.

'I'm not talking to anyone about something as vulgar as money, Raevenne.'

The contempt was cutting enough to slice a person in two. It was credit to Rae that she managed to hold her ground, even if she did conceal a shaky exhale of frustration.

'It's a charity gala. You do understand that asking for money is *exactly* what we're supposed to be doing?'

'We're not doing anything so humiliating,' her mother snapped. 'So you'd better pull your finger out and sort it out yourself. I will not allow you to associate us with a failure.'

'I didn't ask you to associate yourself with it at all,' Raevenne bit out. 'In fact, I don't remember talking to you about it even once. You just decided to throw your names in when Rafe set up the gala and you realised anyone who's anyone in Manhattan was going to be here.'

'Don't whinge, Raevenne. It doesn't suit you. And for that matter, neither does that hideous get-up you're wearing.'

'Oh, I don't know if that's fair, Mummy,' her other sister cut in with the kind of saccharine smile that set Myles' teeth on edge. 'Maybe she's *deliberately* trying to remind the world that she's still that whore from the sex tape.'

He could feel the strength drain out of Rae in the way she sagged against his body, her grip dropping from his arm. He didn't think, didn't hesitate, he simply turned around and wrapped his arm around her to keep her upright.

'I think we're done here, Rae. Let's dance.'

Then, without waiting for a response, he propelled her through the crowd and away from her jealous, vindictive family.

'Put your arm on my shoulder,' he muttered as soon as they were a safe distance away.

It made no sense that her pinched white face should make him feel quite so murderous.

'Raevenne,' he commanded, his voice low and direct. 'Put your hand in mine and your other on my shoulder and dance. Or do you want those witches to win?'

She hesitated, then, as if on autopilot, obeyed his command.

'Good,' he murmured approvingly. 'Now, dance. And smile.'

She managed the first but not the latter.

'Is that what I look like?' her voice finally came out, strangled and quiet. 'Like some kind of...*tart*.'

'You look beautiful,' he growled before he could even think twice. 'Sophisticated, smart, elegant. All the things your grotesque family can only dream of being.'

The twist of her lips could hardly be described as a smile.

'That's the most hypocritical compliment I've heard all night, and, trust me, I've heard a lot of them tonight. I know you hate me, but of course you'd say that. Rafe is paying your salary.'

'That's not why I said it.'

'Of course it is.'

'Look at me, Raevenne. I don't like games and I've no time for people feeling sorry for themselves, so I'm only going to tell you this once. *Look at me.*'

And then she did.

It was like a punch to his lower gut. He wanted to erase every ugly thought she had in her head right at this moment. He wanted to make her see her hideous family for what they were and realise that she was no longer the eighteen-year-old who had made that life-changing video.

He knew his reaction made no sense. He couldn't explain it; worse, he didn't want to. He wasn't sure exactly who *this* Raevenne Rawlstone was, or even if she could really be trusted. All he knew was that he no longer felt as though he was talking to the girl who had humiliated Rafe all those years ago.

'Tell me what, Myles?'

Her voice was barely recognisable, its quiver seeming to mirror all the emotions he was trying to deny were jostling inside him, desperate to get out. He refused to let them, but then she flicked out a tongue to moisten her lips and he was powerless to stop his eyes momentarily dropping to track its progress.

'I didn't want to take this job protecting *you*. I admit it.'

Her expression flickered, like a flame on the verge of being extinguished. He felt even more of a cad.

'Then why did you?' she managed.

'I needed the job,' he stated flatly. 'And Rafe asked me to.'

It was close enough to the truth. How could he tell her that a part of him had welcomed the offer when he'd been ashamed of such a reaction?

'Well, you don't need to worry about it for too much longer,' she managed bitterly, before she could stop herself.

'Which means what, precisely?'

'Forget it. So that's what you wanted to tell me?' Disappointment crept into her voice. 'An admission of something I already knew? That you never wanted to play bodyguard to me?'

He hesitated, assessing her. Evaluating. Or maybe he was evaluating himself. He couldn't be sure. 'Not entirely,' he conceded after a long moment. 'I wanted to apologise.'

'You did?'

'Rafe told me a long time ago that the stories… the stories about you…weren't true, but I didn't believe him. I just couldn't understand why you wouldn't go to the authorities.'

'I told you why the other night.' She was clearly trying not to sound bitter. 'You didn't want to hear it.'

'Would you?' The challenge burst out before he could swallow it. 'Hearing that protecting my reputation and my career was the reason *you* allowed someone like that to use you?'

'So…you believe me?'

Did he? Evidently he must do.

'It isn't easy to change what I thought to be true all this time,' he hedged.

'You're not the only one. It's hard to shatter people's perceptions, especially a bad one they simply love to hate.'

Why did it feel like a victory that he'd swept that sad expression from her features and now a small smile toyed at the corners of her mouth?

Too late, he realised he was bending his neck, almost ready to claim that soft, inviting mouth with those perfectly pink, plump lips. Jerking his head back, he caught himself in time.

'Your family taints everything they're associated with, even a charity event. It's time you distanced yourself from them, Rae, the way Rafe did.'

'I've spent years distancing myself from them,' she cried out.

'Then you need more distance.'

'Trust me, soon enough I won't be able to get any more distance.' She stopped abruptly, biting her lip.

As if she hadn't intended to say anything, as though the admission had tumbled out before she could stop herself.

'Rae?' he prompted, using the tone he'd perfected as an officer. The one that made his men talk to him even when they might have preferred to keep it all inside.

'There's a woman here—' she wrinkled her nose awkwardly '—Angela Kaler, who helped me to organise this charity event. I'm joining her worldwide health programme abroad.'

'Angela Kaler?' he frowned. 'I know her. A few years ago the army sent my unit, a logistics unit and some engineers to join her organisation on one of the hearts and minds missions in a former warzone.'

'Yeah? Well, now she's running humanitarian programmes sending doctors where they're needed, whether conflict zones, or just a remote area in need of a school or a hospital or a well; or where there's been a natural disaster, or maybe an epidemic. I volunteered.'

'*You're* going? What does Rafe say about it?'

'Rafe doesn't know.' She jutted her chin out defiantly, voicing the one thing he didn't want to hear.

'Rae—'

'No.' This time, she refused to cow to him. 'This is something I want to do. I've done all the courses, all the tests, all the evaluations. I passed them all. I got my mission a while ago. Myles, I've been planning it for months…long before he made you shadow me, and long before this latest death threat.'

'Yet you must see that's exactly why you can't now go,' Myles pointed out.

She shook her head wildly, her eyes suddenly dancing with the same kind of light as when she saved a baby. Only now, it was even brighter, even more mesmerising.

'Surely that's even more of a reason to go? If that break-in wasn't opportunistic, and if my life *is* in danger here, they definitely won't be able to get to me where I'm going. I'll be safe, Rafe will be happy, and you'll be free of babysitting me. Everybody wins.'

Only, for a moment, he wasn't sure it felt like a win for him. And he couldn't help feeling Rae felt the same. This…*thing*…still shimmered and rippled between them, however much they pretended to ignore it.

But what was the alternative? That he joined her out there? An invisible band tightened around his chest, making it painful even to draw breath. Images of that village, those bodies, flashed in his brain like flicking through a photo album too quickly to dwell on any single photo, but recognising the images all the same.

His heart picked up its beat, and he fought off the urge to stick a finger between his stiff white collar and his skin. He wasn't ready to go back to a conflict zone. He still hadn't processed what had happened that last mission. The people he'd been laughing with only hours before...

Not to mention the decision he'd made to ignore his gut when he'd discovered that Lance Corporal McCoy—Mikey—was part of the squad that final, fatal time.

It was all he could do to keep looking at Rae, to keep dancing, to keep upright. If he could get through tonight, buy himself enough time, experience told him it would be a lot easier to work things through in the light of the morning. Maybe Rafe was right. Maybe he should have talked to someone.

He just had to get through one night.

Just tonight.

Abruptly, he stopped dancing.

'Where's Angela now?' he demanded.

'Why?' She was understandably guarded and nervous. 'Myles...we've stopped dancing. People are watching.'

'Let them watch.' He didn't care. 'And I'm coming with you.'

Sliding his arm around her, he whisked her around, a weave and a turn and they were back into a decent space.

'That's insane.' She was trying to stay light in his arms, following his lead and floating like a feather. He could tell she felt anything but. 'You can't come. You don't have clearance.'

Something deep in his chest thudded with apprehension. Old fears slowly resurrecting themselves, but he stamped them down.

They had no business in the here and now.

'I was a trauma surgeon in the field six months ago—I have clearance.'

He'd just hoped to never use it again. And yet...

'You can't go into the field within twelve months of being in the forces.' She sounded panicked.

'Some organisations say that,' he acknowledged. 'But not Angela's. Her criteria are different and I fit it. I know that for a fact.'

'You need evaluations.'

'Shall I say it again?' He had no idea why a part of him actually seemed to be thrilling to the concept whilst another part balked. Loudly. 'They're all covered.'

She stared at him, her green eyes wide and shooting sparks.

'This is nonsense, Myles. You have to have a special training for contagious diseases and tropical medicine.'

'I did a year with the Liverpool School of Tropical Medicine in the UK.' He held her tighter, and he couldn't work out who was holding whom upright. 'You can't get rid of me, Rae. I'm coming with you and that's decided.'

'But...'

It was done. He couldn't afford to second-guess. He'd made a commitment to Rafe and he was seeing it through. He wasn't about to let his buddy down. Not even if that meant going back out to hellholes like those with which he was all too familiar. And there was no other reason for his change of heart.

None at all.

'Now, shall we see about getting those donations for you? Let's make this event the best fundraiser these social climbers have ever had the privilege of attending. And as for the rest of your family, they can go and jump in their new handmade rock pool.'

CHAPTER FIVE

HOURS LATER RAE still hadn't processed what Myles had said.

He was coming with her?

It had sounded surreal. But she'd decided that if she just clung to Myles, if she simply stared into those eyes that were so hot, so searing that they seemed to cauterise each lash and wound from the tongues of every single person in this room tonight, then maybe she could emerge from this gala miraculously unscathed, after all.

And so she'd clutched him, physically and mentally, as she worked her way around the room, inch by inch, making sure the night was an unequivocal success. Whether her family tried to take credit for it or not, this night had to be a triumph by securing eye-watering donations from even the Jennings and the Kemps and telling her that the charity deserved nothing less.

Enough to buy container loads of medical supplies, clothing, and heaving toy boxes for the kids. Christmas several times over.

So why did it continue to needle her that he'd shut her out so abruptly back there?

And why did it thrill her when they worked together as though they were some kind of team? Her and Myles against everyone else. Certainly against her family. Gravitating towards each other as they had done a decade earlier. As though it was the most natural thing in the world. As though it was more than just a situation engineered by her half-brother. As though she and Myles were the kind of real couple that everyone who had seen them had assumed them to be. And so she was still clinging onto Myles when he walked her through her door several hours later—the first time she'd returned since the break-in, more relieved than she would ever admit that he and her brother had agreed it wasn't safe enough to leave her alone. Not until they could identify the reason for the break-in.

Still, it didn't stop her from grumbling as she walked along the corridor half an hour later only for Myles to step out of the bathroom. Her nerves were jangling in an effort not to let her eyes drift down the naked, solid, mouth-watering chest. Or to linger on the soft white towel that teasingly just about went around his hips but stopped halfway down his thighs.

She tried to shift. The air seemed to have closed in on her, almost stealing the breath from her lungs. The strange magnetic draw that she'd spent the last few days denying was impossible to ignore now they were stuck in a room...well, a corridor...together. Alone.

All of a sudden her clothes felt too tight for her body and she was sure her tight nipples were visible through the soft tee.

'I still don't understand why this particular death threat has Rafe so rattled. It isn't like we aren't always getting them. He's head of a global company where, no matter how environmentally friendly the design is, new construction is always angering some group or another. My two sisters—not the nicest of people to start with, I'm afraid—live off income from their substantial shares and flaunt it in people's faces via their reality show *Life in the Rawl*, and, as you've reminded me on multiple occasions already, I've got a sex tape out there, which won't go away no matter how many babies I deliver or how many lives I save.'

Something flashed across his features—too

fast for her to put a label on it, and less muted than that first day, but she might have guessed it was disdain.

She told herself it didn't cut through her. That his opinion of her didn't matter any more than that of hundreds, even thousands, of other people out there.

'And is your brother always getting into cars where the brakes have been tampered with?' he asked bluntly.

She reached out for the handrail to steady herself.

'They tampered with Rafe's brakes? He never said.'

'He didn't want to scare you.'

'Whilst you, of course, don't care about that.'

He shrugged, and peered at her and she had the oddest sensation he was trying to see right down to her soul.

Her body and her mind were spiking with desire, and for a moment they stood there, watching each other, not moving. She was desperate to say something, anything, to fill the silence. To give him and his ridiculously tantalising towel a reason not to leave. It made no sense.

Or more worryingly, it made perfect sense.

'You didn't have to do that, tonight,' she managed. 'Help me get donations, I mean. I know I'm not your favourite person.'

'I wanted to.'

'Thank you.'

They stood again, silent and motionless. The tension cranking up a notch. Something inched down her spine and, if she hadn't known better, Rae might have wondered if the thermostats hadn't been set a touch too high. It was paradoxical, then, that she shivered.

She might have known the ever astute Myles wouldn't miss it.

'Cold?'

He hitched one eyebrow. *As though he knew it was pure molten heat burning though her.* She narrowed her eyes.

'A little.'

'Liar,' he whispered.

The wry smile tugged at the corners of his mouth, snagging her gaze, pinning it, and doing things to her insides that he had no business doing. Her stomach couldn't have been more fluttery if it had turned into the lepidoterarium where last year's fundraiser had been held. But infinitely worse than that was the way a fire was roaring deep inside her, much, *much* lower down.

The smouldering embers making heat, and desire, and *need* pool between her legs.

What was the matter with her that she was so incredibly attracted to this man? Even after all these years. He was like an insect that had crawled under her skin and was itching her from the inside out. It made no sense.

She would be wise to remember that Myles had never said that he believed her explanations as to what had happened with Justin, just that it was *difficult to change his perceptions*. And the truth was that he'd never even tried to explain his *own* actions that night he'd rejected her all those years ago. Yet she still felt as if she weren't herself. That she hadn't found herself. Worse, there was no denying the electricity that sparked and arced between her and Myles.

So many years later and she was pretty much in the same position she'd been in all those years ago.

'You know my sisters will give me the third degree next time I see them?' She swallowed hard, trying to loosen her dry tongue. To find something—anything—to say to break the silence. 'They'll want to know exactly how I came to be in contact with you again. And how you came to escort me to that ball.'

'I can't say I give a damn what that lot want to know.'

He took a step towards her, his voice unbelievably husky. Sexy.

She should back away. The idea of something happening between them was insane. And yet she couldn't bring herself to move a muscle. All she could think about was how much she longed to tell him the truth. But that was madness. The whole world had already decided what they knew about her to be true. Whatever she said, Myles wasn't going to believe her.

And did it even matter? In a few days she'd be gone. Thousands of miles away on the month-long posting that she'd told him about earlier that evening.

By the time she returned, Rafe would have resolved the issue of the death threats and life would be back to normal. No more bodyguard. No more Myles.

The last thing she needed to do was complicate it now.

He took another step towards her.

'I'm not who you think I am, you know,' she choked out in panic.

She hated that he pulled a face. She was suddenly so desperate for him to know the truth. As if, if she could convince him that she wasn't the girl the media had set her up to be—had never been that girl, not really, not intentionally—then maybe there was hope she could one day convince the rest of the world.

'Stop, Rae. You were better off when you didn't play that game.'

He was so close now she could almost feel the heat bouncing off his body.

'It isn't a game,' she managed shakily.

'I've seen enough about you over the years to know it's always a game with you lot.' The words were ground out almost as though he was acting against his own will.

And he still didn't step away. He didn't break eye contact.

'Myles—'

'Stop talking,' he bit out.

There was no reason at all for her to obey. *So why did she?*

And then he'd closed the gap completely and they were standing there, in front of each other, and she had no idea what to do next.

Myles, by contrast, suffered no such doubts.

He reached over, thrusting his fingers into her hair and hauling her to him, to his mouth. Then he kissed her.

And, oh, how he kissed her.

He didn't just press his mouth to hers, he claimed her, invaded her, branded her with every slide of his tongue and every graze of his teeth.

Her entire being exploded, like the most dazzling firework display on New Year's Eve. She wasn't sure when she'd lifted her hands but somehow they were on his shoulders, her fingers biting into the thick, corded muscles, revelling in Myles' strength, his size.

Like coming home.

Briefly, images of that awful tape, and the way she'd been with the press those years immediately following the most humiliating year of her life, flooded her brain.

She should tell Myles the truth, she thought weakly. Surely basic pride, self-respect, should mean she'd want him to know who she really was.

But what if he didn't like it?

He'd claimed to despise the brash, indiscreet, classless girl she'd reinvented herself into those years immediately after the sex tape had come out. He'd told her that she epitomised everything he despised. He'd been only too quick to accept the media lies that this was the girl she still, albeit to a moderately lesser extent, was.

Yet here he was. On the one hand telling her that he loathed her. On the other, kissing her as though he couldn't get enough of her. Would *never* get enough of her.

He certainly hadn't kissed the quiet, innocent, pure Raevenne like this.

Which made her wonder which girl he was *really* attracted to.

And then there was the fear that she would tell him what had really happened, and he wouldn't believe her. Sadness spiralled down inside her like the helicopter seed from a sycamore tree.

As much as people were all too eager to accept her first, scandalous reinvention from innocent girl to man-eating, party-loving vamp, it had never suited their salacious appetites to see that only a few years later she'd reinvented herself again into a focussed, private, junior doctor.

It was too deliciously scandalous to keep seeing her as the girl she'd been for those few brief, lost years. The girl who had made a sex tape with her bodyguard to boost her ailing family name, to bring in *money*, after their father's death.

And yet she put up with it. All the press' lies and all the public's feigned shock, because, frankly, she'd wasted enough years trying to win her father's approval when he'd been alive. She'd be damned if she was going to waste more years trying to win over a public who thrived on the perceived drama.

But if Myles did that…? If he refused to see past his prejudice and only saw her as that girl, she feared it would torment her far worse than anything else. *Better not to try or know than to try only to be disappointed.*

Placing her hands on his chest, she braced herself. It was distracting, how little strength she suddenly seemed to have. How instead of pushing him away, her fists were curling around his lapels, and pulling him closer.

Briefly, she wondered where all this was leading.

Would it shock Myles to know that, even though she'd slept with Justin that night because she'd imagined herself to be in love, believed him to be her soul mate, she'd never once felt as *alive* as she had with Myles?

Probably.

Probably worse.

Yet still she clung to Myles, his mouth crushing hers so exquisitely, and hers responding so completely. As though every part of her had been waiting for him to do it all night.

As he kissed his way down her body, searing

her skin with his mouth as he dropped kisses down her neck, across her breasts and nipples, which were so tight they ached, and over her belly, she closed her eyes and let the shivers of pleasure ripple through her body. He might as well have been worshipping every inch of her, and as she stood there, practically naked and otherwise exposed, she realised that he didn't make her feel ashamed, or small, or cornered, the way Justin had.

On the contrary, Myles made her feel powerful, desirable, all woman. It was a heady experience. She'd never ached for *anyone* the way she ached for Myles.

If only she knew how to act on it. How to *show* him.

He was kissing her to prove a point, Myles told himself fiercely. A point to himself. To her. It didn't matter. All that mattered was that he understood that he wasn't kissing her because he hadn't been able to bear another second without doing so.

He wasn't kissing her because his entire body had *ached* for him to do so ever since they'd walked into that ballroom.

No. It was ever since she'd walked into Rafe's offices back in the UK last week.

He couldn't acknowledge that the truth was altogether less complicated and more primal. He mustn't. Because he didn't want to give himself any reason to stop.

'Myles...' She murmured the objection against his lips even as her arms tightened around his body.

A better man would have listened to what she wasn't able to say. A better man would have stopped. A better man would have walked away.

Up until tonight, Myles would have imagined himself to be that man. But right here, right now, he couldn't tear himself away from the kiss. More to the point, he didn't want to,

'Tell me to stop,' he ordered, his lips barely leaving hers. 'Tell me, and I will.'

But it was a safe assurance, because they both knew she couldn't do it. They both knew that she was as consumed by the kiss as he was. As powerless to put an end to it.

Myles' skin prickled. *What was it about this woman that allowed her to get under his skin the way she did?* She was the epitome of everything he despised. Or at least, she had been. The woman he'd been watching these last few days was so different from the caricature he'd thought he'd known. And he certainly hadn't allowed for the inconvenient chemistry that arced undeniably between them.

The chemistry that meant that he was now standing—and he had no idea when or how this had happened—right in front of her with his hands gripping her upper arms, his face dangerously close to hers. A delicate, faintly floral scent filled his nostrils, making his pulse race even faster.

'What…are you doing?'

Her voice was altogether too hoarse, too raw, too…everything, but she didn't pull away. He wondered if she could. Was she as helplessly trapped in her body as he was in his, right now? He could taste her on his lips the way he had back in that ballroom. God, but he wanted to taste her again. His body tightened painfully. His head pounded.

He pulled her closer. She didn't exactly resist.

'Myles…' It was little more than a breathless whisper.

'Tell me I'm wrong. Tell me you haven't been looking at me like this, all night.'

It might sound like a command but it felt like a plea. As though, for the first time in his entire life, Myles didn't feel in control of himself, and knew that he wasn't going to be able to walk away from her this time.

'I...' She faltered, her gaze flicking from his eyes to his mouth and back again.

Her tongue darted out to wet her mouth and the last of his resolve began to crumble. Desperate need gripped him.

Without warning, Rae crested up onto her tiptoes and pressed her lips to his, the grudging mutter vibrating on his mouth.

'You can pretend all you like, but you want me just as badly.'

And everything else tumbled. Need and desire ripped through him. As lethal an ambush as any he'd known out of the battlefield, almost dropping him where he stood.

He hauled her to him, revelling in the way every inch of her delicious body moulded itself to every inch of his, her hands reaching up to wind around his neck, her head angling to allow him better access.

He tasted her, plundered her mouth, losing himself in the maelstrom of desire that had been swirling inside him from the first moment they'd met again in the Rawlstone Group's HQ, however much he'd tried to deny it.

Slowly, carefully, he ran his hands down her body, over the rough, metallic beads of her slinky, sexy dress, until he reached the high slit on her thigh. He should take it slower, take his time, but he couldn't. He was driven by the primal need to divest her of her clothing and bury himself inside her, so deep, so tight, that neither of them would know where one ended and the other began.

So, instead, he slid his hand inside, easing the dress enough that when he lifted her up, she could wrap her legs around his waist, her perfect heat pressed against the very hardest part of himself. And then he released the clasps that kept the halter neck in place, letting them drop, and it felt as though the very air were sucked from his lungs as he took in the soft swell of gloriously creamy skin; the deliciously hard, brown buds that strained as if in a greeting meant only for him.

Briefly he recalled the images he'd seen of her, a lot more naked than this, a lot more compromised than this. With any other woman it would have been enough to stop him. To put him off. It should concern him more that it didn't. But Rae was such a different woman from the girl in that sex tape. So far removed from the girl who'd been linked to more men than he'd had ration-packed army meals.

He desired her, ached for her, and there wasn't a damned thing he seemed to be able to do about it. He looked into her eyes, all the longing and the need he felt reflected back at him. He shifted and her breath hitched, making him feel more powerful than he'd ever felt. So, for once in his life, Myles shut his brain off, stopped trying to tell himself that he should know better, and instead let his body do the thinking.

Why not? What harm could it do?

He backed them against a wall, her legs still locked around him and one hand still cradling her pert backside, whilst the other explored. His palm grazed her skin as his thumb raked over one taut nipple. She gasped, her eyes slightly hooded, her cheeks slightly pink, but not breaking her gaze from his. He tried it again, and this time she rocked her body so that it pressed harder against him, sending need pulsing all through him.

He cupped her tighter, letting his mouth take over from where his hand had been. His tongue swirling gently around the nipple, revelling in the way her breathing shallowed, then sucking hard until she cried out with pleasure.

* * *

Rae opened her mouth to speak only to find she couldn't say a word. He was cupping her, her sex chafing on the lacy material that he hadn't even bothered to remove. She gasped and rocked against him, his palm raking over her wet heat. His eyes not leaving hers, he twisted his hand, and suddenly he was on the other side of the lace, tracing her swollen folds with almost lazy ease. She shivered and moved against him, desperate to intensify the pleasure, but he shifted his hand away, his mouth curling into a teasing smile.

'I'll be the one setting the pace, I think, Rae-venne, not you.'

And she groaned and gasped, her fingers biting into his solid shoulders, trying to obey him, yearning for him to begin again. The way he was taking his time was like some exquisite torture. It hadn't been like this her one time before. As if she could go on for ever, yet simultaneously couldn't wait another second.

As if he could read her mind, Myles drew his finger around her again, but this time, as he closed the pattern, he moved his finger straight across her core, stroking the most sensitive bud. Fast then slow, then fast again, repeating it, deepening it, until she felt dizzy, almost mindless. This time, when she surged against his hand, he didn't stop. Instead he matched her, pulled her along with him, her body clenching and fizzing and burning with this fire he was building, as his mouth now paid homage to her neck, his teeth nipping at her earlobes, pressing kisses into the sensitive hollow behind her ear.

Without warning, he moved his hand away, and it took Rae every ounce of strength to lift her head.

'Don't stop,' she gasped, not realising she'd uttered the words until Myles answered her. His voice was thick with desire, his thumb pressed to his lips.

'I have no intention of stopping.'

'Please...'

'I have no intention of this night ending any time soon.'

Suddenly his hand was back, his cold thumb pad taking up where his fingers had left off, the pace every bit as powerful, as intense as before. The sensations were cresting now, threatening to crash down over her, like nothing she'd ever known before. She was gripping his shoulders tighter, barely recognising the sounds escaping her as she began to buck against his hand. And as everything began to explode in her head, throughout her body, he slid his finger inside her, then another, his thumb maintaining the deliciously punishing pace. Rae shattered.

She was only half aware of burying her head in his shoulder to keep from crying out his name so loudly that anyone outside her room might hear. And still Myles didn't stop. Without warning, he twisted his wrist and the last of the explosions sounded in her head, and then she was soaring and tumbling, and there was silence. Pure, blissful silence.

She finally came back to herself to find him watching her. The unguarded look in his eyes pierced straight through her, making her heart do strange looping things in her chest.

You're falling for him, you little idiot.

The voice sounded remarkably like the sharp, bitter mocking of any one of her sisters.

You're a fool if you think this is anything more than just sex to him.

She blanched, hating it, and tried to thrust it aside. But not quickly enough, it seemed, and before she could think twice she was bracing against him, pulling away.

'Rae.' The warning was unmistakeable, but she pretended she couldn't hear it.

She couldn't afford to hear it.

She wanted him inside her. So much that it was almost painful. She wanted him to take her, to show her all the things she'd read about, heard about, but which Justin had ruined for her. The reason why she couldn't bring herself to utter the words aloud, however much they hovered on her lips, or hummed through her body.

'Is that it?' she heard herself demand, her cool, brittle voice nothing she'd ever sounded like before. 'The best you've got?'

'Say again?'

Something dark and lethal moved between them but she only jerked her head up higher and ignored it. There was no other way. She couldn't have sex with Myles. If that was how much he made her come apart just from touching her, if that was how easy it had been to break her defences and remember just how much she'd loved him in her girlish, naïve way, then she could only imagine how intense it would be to have full-on sex with him.

She couldn't risk it. She couldn't be hurt again by him.

Not like last time.

'I must say, I've had better.' Every word scratched inside her. 'I was expecting more from you.'

'What the hell kind of game are you playing, Raevenne?'

His low voice was like a physical blow but she stood her ground, though she would never know how.

'Talk about an anticlimax.' It was amazing how still her hands were as they made a great show of sorting her clothes out, deliberately, unashamedly, with no indication of just how much she was shaking inside.

'Well, as…enlightening as that was, Myles…' *think airy, think breezy, don't think needy* '… I really don't feel we need to revisit it, do you? And, for both our sakes, let's never speak of it again.'

CHAPTER SIX

'WHAT HAVE WE GOT?'

Rae barely had time to glance at the interpreter, Clara, as her colleagues brought in a heavily pregnant young woman, clearly in pain and looking generally unwell. She gazed at the doctors with a mix of fear and hope.

Just like the hundreds of pregnant women and babies Rae had already seen in the five days since she'd arrived at the camp, none of whom had ever been under the care of a doctor in their life before.

It was a never-ending flood of desperate women, all with pregnancy or labour complications. But then, that was the issue out here. Lack of nearby medical services, lack of money for medicine, or being a displaced person meant that non-complicated pregnancies were dealt with at home. They either never came into the clinic in the first instance, or they only came in when they realised there was a problem—often, sadly, when it was too late.

And so the place was heaving with pregnant women who needed medical attention. Rae was already beginning to realise that an average twenty-four-hour period here meant sixty or seventy women giving birth and many of them—so many of them—needing emergency C-sections at the very least.

She felt as if she was stretched so thin she was terrified of missing something.

There was one silver lining, though. And that meant the shifts were so long, so exhausting, that it was all Rae could ever do to stumble back to her room in the compound and flop onto her cot bed and into sleep—a deep sleep, not plagued by memories of that night with Myles. Certainly not reliving the excruciating awkwardness of the flight over here, when they had scarcely been able to look at each other, let alone exchange a civil word.

Even now she could feel her cheeks heating at the memory of that night together. Or, *not together*, depending on how she looked at it. The way he'd touched her, made her come alive in a way no one ever had before... Her heart skittered slightly in her chest. And then the way it had all unravelled in those final, humiliating moments…

'This is Fatima.' The interpreter mercifully drew Rae back to the present. 'She's twenty-six. She has severe pain on her right side and has suffered some blood loss. She's about eight months pregnant and she has been walking with her husband for several days, almost non-stop, to get here.'

'Is this her first baby?'

Rae carefully examined the young woman as Clara translated the question and Fatima replied earnestly between her gasps of pain.

'Yes,' Clara passed the information on, 'although she's had a couple of early-term miscarriages in the past.'

'I take it Fatima hasn't seen a doctor throughout this pregnancy?'

She knew the answer, but she still had to ask the question, just as Clara had to check.

'No one,' Clara confirmed after a moment.

'There's a strong foetal heartbeat.' Rae nodded, using the handheld Doppler device. 'That's a good sign. Still, I'd like to take her through for a proper ultrasound.'

No need to mention her concern over the solid mass under Fatima's ribs. Not until the ultrasound confirmed her suspicions that it was the baby's head, and that the baby was lying transverse, instead of head down.

As she waited for the only machine they had to become free, Rae watched the couple as the man held his wife's hand. Caring, loving, tender. It was touching, not least because it was so different from many of the cases over the last few days.

Back home, she was so accustomed to talking to the mother-to-be, ensuring the woman gave consent for herself. Yet out here she was already beginning to learn that the women rarely made their own choices. So many times already she'd found herself conflicted when she'd spoken to the woman only for the woman to look straight to her husband or even her husband's mother, to be told what she could or could not do.

If Rafe were here, she could have talked to him. She hadn't realised quite how much she'd come to rely on bouncing ideas back and forth with her half-brother over the last few years. She could talk to any of the other volunteers, of course. She knew that. But instead her thoughts came squarely back round to Myles.

As they so often had since that night.

Since before that night, a voice echoed in her

head. *Since the moment you walked into Rafe's offices and saw Myles standing there.*

It was impossible to escape him. Not physically, since he'd clearly been keeping his distance this last week, but mentally. Neither of them had mentioned the kiss, the…sex, but memories of it pervaded her thoughts constantly, even when she didn't want them to.

Especially, it seemed, because she didn't want them to. And even those mere echoes were enough to make her body shiver and pulse, and feel more alive than she had done in such a painfully long time.

Or ever.

Which was as terrifying as it was thrilling since it called into question everything she'd thought was true the night she'd let Justin convince her that she was ready to lose her virginity to him.

The night she'd told herself that if she was in love with Justin the way she thought she was, then she shouldn't keep holding herself back from sleeping with him. The night she'd told herself that if she didn't want to then perhaps she really was as frigid as her sisters and Justin mocked her for being.

She'd spent the years afterwards believing that

was the only explanation. And then Myles had come along and she'd physically ached for him in a way she'd never known was possible. That night she hadn't had to talk herself into anything with Myles. She'd wanted him with such a wanton intensity that surely no one could ever have felt before.

She should have been ashamed—living up to every last false image that had been told about her over the last decade. But Myles had made her feel so...*alive*, so *free*, so powerful. It had been like nothing else she had ever imagined. Nothing like Justin. How could she regret that?

So she'd spent the past few days here desperately ignoring him. She'd got away with it so far, but she couldn't avoid him for ever. Not if she didn't want the other volunteers to notice and start wondering. She and Myles had arrived together; it would be obvious if she avoided him for the entire month.

As she'd heard at least three times already this shift, even in a place as hellish as this it couldn't be all work, *all* the time. There had to be at least a few moments of snatched private time, or else one would go truly insane.

Which meant once her shift ended, she was

going to have to go and find him and come up with a solution.

She told herself that it was purely apprehension that made her chest spin like the triple-axle she'd learned to execute as a youth champion ice-skater.

'Machine's free.'

Rae stared blankly for a moment, the words taking their time to sink in, to push away the unwanted thoughts of Myles. And then she was moving, grateful to be able to focus on her patient.

The ultrasound confirmed her suspicion, and since the baby was clearly intent on coming out that night, one way or another, there was nothing else for it but to carry out an emergency C-section.

As Clara translated all the information and gained consent from the mother, Rae looked around for one of the senior surgeons to brief.

'I can join you, if you like,' offered Janine, a sixth-time volunteer and one of Rae's mentors. 'I've just cleared a clinic of the usual diarrhoea and urinary tract infections. I have a free half-hour.'

'That would be brilliant.' Rae nodded gratefully. 'I knew the lack of healthcare out here meant complicated pregnancies were more common than I was used to, but I don't think I was prepared for sixty to seventy women giving birth in a twenty-four-hour period. And many of them to twins or triplets because of the unregulated fertility pills out here.'

'No one is ready that first time.' Janine laughed. 'But you'll get used to it and be a dab hand before you know it. And wait for a busy night when north of ninety women give birth and there are a couple of quadruplets thrown in for an added kick.'

'Oh, well, thanks for that.'

'Any time. Seriously though, Raevenne, you've already settled in well these last few days. You'll be fine. Come on, you take the lead on this one, I'll just assist.'

And then it was time.

Sucking in a steadying breath, Rae lifted the scalpel and began.

'I'm going for a transverse abdominal incision, given the position of the baby.' She cut carefully until she could see the uterus.

But it wasn't what she'd expected and it didn't make any sense. She stopped, frowning. A glance at her equally baffled mentor didn't help. They began a quick set of checks.

'It *is* the uterus,' she breathed a few moments later. Half a statement, half a question.

'It is,' Janine concurred.

'But it looks like a normal, non-pregnant uterus? Yet I felt the baby. I saw it on the ultrasound?'

'Try extending the incision upwards. Until it's T-shaped.'

Dutifully, Rae cut until she was where the gall-bladder might usually be. Only it wasn't a gall-bladder.

'It's an abdominal pregnancy,' they both gasped at once.

Rae shook her head in awe. How was it possible that this baby had developed entirely outside the uterus? Entirely inside the abdominal cavity?

Ectopic pregnancies might occur one or two per cent of the time, but in pretty much all those cases the pregnancy was usually in the fallopian tubes, and would be terminated because of the high risk to the mother. But to see a baby—an almost full-term baby—still alive, outside both the uterus *and* the fallopian tubes? Rae had been prepared for the high number of complications out here, but she could never have imagined she would ever see something like this.

'I've only ever read about this in my medical

journals back home,' she marvelled. 'And even then there was only a sketch to accompany the condition. It's just extraordinary.'

'Once in a lifetime,' agreed Janine. 'And if we're somehow able to get this baby safely out whilst keeping Mum well, I think it will stay with me as the most incredible birth of my career.'

'Do you think we can?' Rae bit her lip. 'Save the mother and the baby?'

'We can certainly try. The baby is crying, so I'd say that was a good sign. We're going to have to get it out as quickly as we can. You see that mass there? That's the placenta. We need to remove it carefully so as not to cause bleeding.'

They worked swiftly, carefully, with one eye on the baby and another on the mother. Both of whom seemed to be doing remarkably well.

Rae wasn't even sure she was breathing during the entire painstaking procedure. But suddenly they were closing up and it was all over and she and Janine stared at each other in disbelief. Tired but elated.

'We'll still have to keep a close eye on them. The mother is at risk of both bleeding and infection, and I don't know how the baby is going to develop, but you should be very proud of yourself, Rae. That's an incredible job tonight.'

'Thank you.' She smiled, not sure whether it was the baby they'd just delivered or her mentor's praise that was filling her with such an incredible sense of euphoria.

'Right, now didn't your shift end an hour and a half ago? So go and get something to eat, get some rest, and we'll do it all again tomorrow. Well, maybe not *this*, exactly.'

'No.' Rae laughed, feeling exhausted but insanely proud. 'Not exactly.'

She wasn't sure whether she crawled, walked or floated to the doors of the clinic but she might have known her escape wouldn't have been that easy as a frantic-looking colleague from the general hospital on the other side of the courtyard came racing in.

'We've got an old guy hauled out of the river. Don't know how long he was down but he was in a bad way. We've run out of stuff. Have you got any blankets and fresh trousers over here?'

She should keep walking. Her shift was over but her next one would start in a matter of twelve hours.

Rae glanced over her shoulder. Everyone was

hectic, as always, and time clearly wouldn't be on the old man's side if he had hypothermia.

'I'm just coming off shift. If you fill out one of your department's authorisation slips I'll run it to the warehouse for you.'

The issue sheets were a precious commodity around here. There was no way the women's clinic could afford to use one of their own for goods from the main hospital, and the warehouse staff couldn't release anything—clothing, food, toiletries—without a paper trail.

'Oh, would you, doll?' the older woman breathed gratefully. 'I'll fill out a slip now. We're swamped over there.'

Rae followed her back across the courtyard, the paperwork in her hands within a minute, a quick, tight hug almost squeezing the life out of her.

A quick run to the stores and back, and then that would be it. Bed. Sleep. And a good breakfast. Then another non-stop twelve-hour shift would start. To so many people, this would be their idea of hell.

Yet somehow, Rae had never felt so settled. So right. As if this was somehow her calling, she just hadn't realised it before.

Her first week would soon be up. Already. Another three and she'd be home. In time for New Year, Rafe had said.

Why did she already get the feeling that one month out here simply wouldn't be enough?

'Oh. I didn't know you'd be here.'

Myles stilled in his task as her voice carried in the quiet, cool air, its faint quiver hitching curiously in his chest.

He battled to keep images of that last evening at her house out of his head. He couldn't afford to go there. Each time he did, something else kicked lower, harder, and eminently more forcefully.

He'd spent five days—seven, if he included the flights over here—pretending he hadn't given in to the temptation of kissing her, tasting her, touching her.

But it was impossible. Rae was always there, tempting him in gloriously vivid Technicolor, whether in his nightly dreams or his waking hours.

He supposed he should be grateful. If he wasn't dreaming of Rae then it was other memories that pervaded his head. Nightmares that infiltrated his sleep like an unwanted invader. Images he could never, ever bury, and which would haunt him for ever.

The longer he'd been out here, the worse they'd become. But he couldn't speak to anyone. He would not talk about it. He was just waiting to get home.

This month out here couldn't end soon enough.

'What are you doing in here, Rae?' He deliberately made his voice unwelcoming, forbidding even, brutally calling to mind every scurrilous thing he'd ever heard or read about her. He couldn't fall for her act again. He *wouldn't*. 'The warehouse is off-limits.'

'I need a couple of blankets, and a pair of trousers for a patient.'

'Authorisation slip?' He held out his hand, taking care not to let their fingers come into contact as she handed it over.

Rae looked exhausted...but elated. He peered at her whilst appearing to be focussed on the paper in his hand.

He'd spent the last week overseeing her from afar, making sure she was safe just as he'd assured Rafe he would do, but he'd kept away. Waiting for her to finally admit that this latest stunt was a step too far; that she was out of her league with the game she was playing with the media; that she'd overestimated her hand in trying to improve her image by coming out to a place like this to volunteer.

Because a place like this ate into your soul. The poverty, the sickness, the pain. He recognised it only too well from his years of operational tours. Indeed, this was tame compared to some of the horrific places he'd visited; missions he'd been a part of.

But it was still eating him alive.

For someone as pampered as Raevenne Rawlstone, it should certainly have been enough to send her screaming back to New York, and the best, cushiest, private practice posting that Rafe's contacts could buy her.

Instead, she was fitting into life out here in a way he'd never anticipated. She hadn't folded, crumbled, or run to contact her brother to get her a way out of here because she couldn't cope, but rather she'd taken a deep breath, rolled her sleeves up, and thrown herself into chaotic camp life.

Which only made it all the more difficult for him to keep his distance. She was like some kind of breathtaking, beautiful angel. But a beauty, he had to remind himself, that only went skin-deep.

'I still don't understand why the clothes have to

sit in this place under lock and key, when there are people out there who need them.'

He told himself not to react to her sad expression.

'Because there aren't enough to go around,' he answered simply. 'If we hand them out now to some families and not to others, we'd have fighting on our hands. That's why all this stuff stays here. Trousers, shoes, tees, whatever. Once we have enough for each family, we'll distribute them.'

'I guess.' She chewed her lip. 'But some families are clearly in greater need than others.'

'Which is why the forward camp near the border gives a basic package to every family coming through their gates.' He shrugged as he located the crate, taking out a couple of pairs of trousers. 'It's the best we can do. Certainly the fairest way we can do it. Which one is closest to his size?'

'Probably that one.' She pointed. 'Have you got a belt?'

He snorted.

'You're not shopping in one of your designer stores now. There's some twine over there. Cut a length off, that will have to do.'

He told himself he didn't notice when she wrinkled her nose and offered him an involuntary sheepish smile. Nor did he notice when she shifted awkwardly from one foot to the other with that little finger-twist tell of hers.

'Myles, I... I wanted to apologise for...you know...that night last week. I—'

There was no reason whatsoever for anything to lance through him the way that it did.

'Forget it,' he cut her off briskly, deliberately focussing on the task in hand.

He tracked across the warehouse.

'Myles...'

He thrust the blankets at her before getting her to sign the authorisation slip and giving her the bottom copy. Then he moved off, ostensibly to find a new bag of donations to sort through and filter into pallet boxes, but she shuffled along behind him.

'I don't want to hear it, Raevenne.'

For a moment he thought she might have stopped. Turned away. And then she spoke again, quietly, urgently.

'I *need* to apologise for that night, Myles. I wasn't...it wasn't...that wasn't me, that night.'

'Don't you need to get those blankets and trousers to your patient?'

She stared down, as if she couldn't remember how the garment had got into her hand in the first place. Then she jerked her head in some semblance of a nod and, muttering something he couldn't catch, hurried out of the repository as quickly as she could.

Which was a good thing, he repeated. Over and over. As if somehow he thought that might make it all the more believable.

He certainly wasn't prepared for her to walk back into the place minutes later, trouser-free.

'Raevenne,' he cautioned, but this time there was no hesitation.

She strode up to him, so close he could smell her unique scent. Whatever objections he'd been about to make erased themselves from his brain.

'Everything is at the hospital where it needs to be, so now I'm back here and you have no more excuses to push me away.'

'Then how about I'm more direct?' he growled, but she stood her ground.

'Please, Myles. I need you to know that I'm not the woman you think I am.'

'You said that once before. I was even ready to believe you, even to believe that maybe your refusal to defend yourself all these years really was out of some kind of misguided loyalty. And then you turned around the other night with that...

stunt, and proved to me you were *exactly* the woman I'd thought you were.'

He tried to sound hostile. He hadn't thought he'd succeeded but then she swallowed once, twice, squeezing her eyes closed as if to summon up all her courage.

'What happened the other night…my reaction…was in part down to the mistake I made all those years ago, with Justin.'

Some unidentifiable emotion surged through him.

'We've already been through this, Rae. I don't want to hear it again.'

'And I don't particularly want to have to say it.' Anger flared in her unexpectedly. 'But I can't seem not to because, frankly, I'm sick of you treating me like I'm some kind of nineteenth-century fallen woman whilst you're completely blame-free.'

'I don't believe either of those things,' he said through what felt like a mouth full of gravel. 'But need I remind you that you were the one who reacted to intimacy between us by telling me that you'd had better?'

'Like I just admitted, I reacted badly, for which I've spent the last few days trying to apologise,' she bit out. 'Which you'd know if you stopped ignoring me for one moment. So I'm just going to keep making these ugly little scenes, which are embarrassing the both of us, until you shut up and listen.'

He eyed her curiously, telling himself that it wasn't hope that made his heart thud in his chest. It wasn't desire that whispered down his spine.

He believed in loyalty and principles, and discretion. She believed in living larger than life, and in letting every last detail of her life be played out in full view of the press and the public. There wasn't a thing about her that the entire world didn't already know.

And yet he couldn't help it. Despite every fibre of his being bellowing at him not to show any weakness, not to cave, the whisper of need infiltrated his head, scraping around in there, like metal on dry ice.

A traitorous part of him wanted to listen to her.

'Fine, you have my full attention.'

She inclined her head a fraction, all elegant grace. Only the red stain creeping up her neck betrayed her.

'I panicked, pure and simple. What happened between us the other night happened so fast and I was embarrassed, because the truth is that I haven't actually slept with anyone since Justin.'

CHAPTER SEVEN

HE WASN'T SURE how long they stood in silence. He only knew that he could barely get a word out for the jumble of questions tripping over themselves on his tongue, and that his heart seemed to hang in his chest. Whether it had forgotten how to beat, or simply didn't have the strength to in that moment, Myles couldn't be sure.

'Say that again?' he managed at last.

'I think you heard me the first time.'

Her soft voice electrified him. He had to take another few moments to get his head around what she was saying.

'You're telling me,' he began huskily, 'that aside from the other night, the only time you've been...*intimate* with a man was the night you made the sex tape with your sleaze of a bodyguard.'

His needling was deliberate. He couldn't seem to help himself. But when she flinched he felt like a heel. Still, she held her head up.

'That's exactly what I'm saying, yes.'

'And you expect me to believe that?'

Something flashed through her eyes for a split second before she shut it down. It shocked Myles to realise that he recognised it as regret.

'I expect that you probably won't. But I didn't ask you to. I simply asked you to listen to me.'

'So you could make out that I was no better than that pervert bodyguard of yours?'

But what really rattled him was the realisation that, if what she was saying were true, then it was all too accurate a description.

Her face might as well have been on fire but to her credit she didn't drop her gaze. If anything, she tilted her head a little higher.

'That's not at all what I'm saying. You're nothing like him. I knew exactly what was happening between you and me, but I didn't have a clue what he was doing.'

'He was making a name for himself,' Myles snarled. 'That's what he was doing.'

'Yes, thank you. Well, that became clear *after* the fact.'

She threw her hands up in the air, her composure slipping, and to Myles' shock he realised that his fury was aimed more at the slimy Justin than at Rae.

'Did you love him?' He didn't know why he even asked.

It didn't matter. He didn't care. It was just some morbid curiosity, surely?

'I… I wanted to love him.' For the first time she allowed her eyes to slide away. 'He told me he loved me and I believed him.'

'Why?'

She snapped her gaze back up to glare at him, making Myles feel as though he was missing something obvious.

'Why do you think, Myles? Because I *wanted* to believe him. The idea of someone loving me, *me*, was so thrilling. For years the boys I'd known had only ever been able to talk about my sisters, how glamourous, or sexy, or hot they were. And then here was Justin paying attention to me, and I fell for it.'

He wanted to tell her that not everyone she'd known had been so taken with her superficial sisters that they'd overlooked the real thing standing right in front of them. To point out to her how close he'd come to being with her that New Year's Eve.

But voicing something like that would be tantamount to knowingly walking out onto quicksand. The consequences were inevitable. So instead he bit back the words and stayed silent.

'I suppose I found it flattering,' Rae continued with a self-deprecating laugh. 'And hearing someone tell me they loved me was like balm to my battered ego. Not least after I'd humiliated myself the night I offered myself to you only for you to throw me out of your bedroom.'

'Christ, Rae, you blame me for humiliating you simply because I had enough respect for you not to sleep with you when you were my best mate's seventeen-year-old kid sister?'

'That wasn't what you said, though, was it?' she fired back. 'You said that I was insane if I thought you were ever going to sleep with me.'

Instantly, shamefully, he recalled his harsh words and the way he'd thrown that handmade quilt from his guest bed over her practically naked form and bundled her out into the corridor in wholly ungentlemanly fashion.

Ironic then, that he'd thought he *was* being gentlemanly by not sleeping with her.

'You were seventeen. I was twenty-one.'

'So? That's perfectly legal. Plus, I was a few months off being eighteen and you were only just twenty-one. There's barely three years between us.'

'It might not have been illegal but it still wouldn't have been a good idea,' he bit out stiffly.

Which made it sound logical, and well thought-out. But the truth was that his decision back then had been less about logic and more about convincing himself to keep his hands off her than anything else.

At twenty-one, he'd never before experienced such a heady, all-consuming attraction before. His teenage years had been too focussed on dragging himself out of the hellhole of his childhood, trying to build some kind of real future for himself. He'd had a couple of girlfriends but nothing that had amounted to anything much.

And then he'd met Rae and their attraction, their chemistry, had been instantaneous. Overwhelming. Even despite the handful of women with whom he'd been in relationships over the years since then, none of them had equalled the same intense heat he felt with Rae.

Not that he was about to tell her that now. He could already feel that familiar desire stoking up his senses. But he was here under her half-brother's employ to look out for her. He wasn't here to revisit old temptations.

'And you think I'll buy into all this?' He let out a bitter laugh.

Anything to cover the fact that he pretty much already had.

'I know how it sounds, but it's true. I swear it.' She stepped towards him, her hands reaching out instinctively to lie flat on his chest before she caught herself, no doubt expecting him to back away.

He probably should.

He didn't.

And when she tentatively made contact, it was like throwing a match on a pile of dry, petrol-doused leaves. His whole body ignited in an instant. He remembered everything with startling vividness. Her scent, her taste, the way she'd come apart so perfectly with him. He wanted to make her lose herself all over again. To take back every lie that had slipped from her lips. To make her admit she was as hungry for him as he was for her.

He wanted to bury himself inside her, so deep that neither of them would know where one ended and the other began, and he wanted to make her climax all around him. His name the only thing in her head.

But he couldn't do any of that. He couldn't allow himself such a weakness. And it was all he could do not to let her see his reaction.

'What about the *not living up to expectations*?' he growled, trying to remind himself as much as remind her.

She flushed, a deep, scarlet stain spreading over her skin.

'I was embarrassed, Myles. You'd just made me...you know...'

'Orgasm?' he supplied.

If it was possible she flushed an even richer hue. It didn't help his self-control one bit.

'From just a touch,' she muttered.

Awareness rippled through him. He shut it down.

'Which you're now telling me was the only time you've been intimate with a man since you made that vile tape?' he stated flatly, belying the uproar in his head. His chest.

She jerked her head up and down.

'Really? Raevenne Rawlstone, the woman who changes her man along with her always up-to-date seasonal wardrobe.'

Sarcasm was etched into every syllable of the well-bandied media quote.

Rae stared at him for a moment, her eyes dulling.

'You don't believe me.'

He wanted to believe her. With an urgent, *pri-*

mal drive he'd only ever felt with this one woman; with a voice that roared that she was *his*. That she'd always been his.

Ever since he'd made her come apart in his arms barely a week ago. Even then hadn't he wondered at her sweetness, her naivety, her lack of experience? Right up until the moment she'd pulled her *'is that it?'* charade and it had been easier to despise her for that than to consider she might have been saving herself all these years? For him?

'You surely can't believe for a second that I'll buy into this *prim* act of yours?' he bit out icily, hating himself for the less than proper thoughts racing through his body.

Taking up residence in his sex as surely as if she'd skimmed her hand over him.

'Why not? Because you know me so well?' Her boldness was a delicious challenge. 'Are you really so entrenched that you can't begin to even consider that there might be some truth in what I'm saying? Or is there a part of you that can't allow yourself to believe me because then you might have to finally acknowledge that we're attracted to each other? Still.'

'This conversation is pointless, Rae,' he warned, but she ignored him.

'Just as we were attracted to each other over a decade ago. Only back then I was gullible enough to believe you when you said you didn't want me. This time, I think we both know the truth.'

He stood immobile, rooted to the spot and unable to move even if he'd tried. Never mind his legs, though, it was all he could do to get his mouth moving.

'I'm your bodyguard, Rae.'

'That didn't stop you the other night,' she whispered. 'Besides, did you really need to come to this with me? We still don't know if that break-in at my house was merely opportunistic, but even if it wasn't, surely no one is going to reach me thousands of miles away?'

'Actually, we *do* know about the break-in.' He hadn't known whether to tell her or not before she'd brought it up herself. 'From their investigation at the house and everything that you confirmed was taken, they've concluded there is more than likely a connection between the break-in at your home and the tampering of Rafe's brakes.'

'Which means whoever it is is operating on both sides of the Atlantic?'

She paled, her scratchy voice worming into

him and making him wish he could do something, anything, to take away her fear.

'There is an upside.' He would never know how he sounded so detached, so in control, when every word felt clunky and awkward, as though his brain was trying to work out how to piece words together. How to make a sentence. 'In that it also narrows the field considerably. Not many individuals have that kind of reach.'

'You're thinking competitors to Rawlstone Group? Were they trying to get to Rafe through me?'

The idea of Rae being in danger, of him having to voice it aloud, filled him with something he didn't care to evaluate too closely.

'It's too early to say for certain, but that's certainly one line of investigation we're currently following.'

She swallowed.

'Which means they *could* reach me here. If they really wanted to.'

'It's unlikely.' He forced his voice to become lighter than he really felt. 'But it can't be ruled out.'

'We have three more weeks here. Together,' she managed. As if she could somehow pretend that the last half-hour hadn't happened. 'So we have to get past this. Get along with each other.'

'You do know I will protect you, Rae?'

'From any external dangers, yes.' She looked as though she wanted to say something else, something more, but eventually she offered a resigned shrug.

'We've managed to keep our distance up until now. Perhaps we can just carry on like that?'

'It won't work. The last few days have been hectic but as the new teams settle in we're going to have to spend more time together. It would look odd if we didn't.'

Her body slumped as though suddenly leaden.

'What are you suggesting?'

'That we find a truce. Any animosity between us would quickly filter through the camp and bring the rest of the volunteers down. So perhaps we should...forget our history. Start again.'

'Start again?' She looked dubious. 'How, precisely, are we supposed to do that?'

He hadn't thought that far. His whole adult life he'd had a plan, had mapped things out in advance. He liked it that way. He thrived on being prepared. But now his mind cast around wildly until, eventually, it touched on a potential solution and grasped it as though it were the last life jacket and he were on a sinking ship.

'Christmas. Come on, I'll show you.'

'Christmas?' She frowned.

It was galling how contained, how unaffected Myles was whilst her heart was skittering around her chest and her thoughts were a chaotic mess.

Just like that New Year's Eve back when she'd been seventeen.

She forced the past from her head and fought to concentrate on the here and now.

'Yes,' Myles was announcing, his tone clipped. 'Your Christmas toy boxes have arrived.'

'Really?'

She hadn't expected his tactics to work, but suddenly a thread of excitement rippled through her as she hurried after him across the warehouse. And then she saw the pallet boxes, the contents wrapped in a transparent film, and she stopped dead.

It was almost surreal. The same red, white and green boxes that had been filled in New York were now out here, and her fingers longed to reach out and lift the pop-up Christmas tree on just one of them.

'I can't believe they're here,' she murmured. 'I can't believe *I'm* here.'

The excitement rippled again. And then something else. She wasn't prepared for the apprehension that suddenly overcame her, like a fire blanket thrown down to smother the flames.

'Everything okay?'

As if he could read her thoughts.

Her eyes flickered to his almost against his will.

'What was I thinking?' she murmured.

'Rae?'

'There I was, back in my sheltered life in New York, going on and on about these boxes, encouraging people to come to a charity gala just to donate for more boxes, for toys, for Christmas, when the kids out here don't need that. I was naïve. I didn't have a clue what it was really like to be a kid out here. I've wasted so much time on stuff which doesn't matter.'

'It *does* matter, Raevenne.'

'Of course it doesn't. I was such an idiot, telling people how important those toy boxes were, back home. Making such a big deal out of getting people to buy them or fill them.'

'You're not an idiot.'

'Of course I am,' she cried. 'As if Christmas means the same thing out here. The kids out here don't need stupid toys, they need real solutions for real problems, like where their next meal is coming from, whether the water is safe enough to drink, if their mother is going to get through her next childbirth without a fatal complication.'

She was so caught up in her own frustration that she didn't notice Myles reach out until he'd snagged her hand, holding it tightly in his.

'What are you doing?'

'Come with me.'

It was a command rather than a request. And one that, despite everything, Rae found herself obeying.

'Have you actually been around the camp since you arrived?'

'A little.' She wrinkled her nose.

The truth was she'd been so caught up in getting herself up to speed medically that she really hadn't had time to go anywhere but the clinic, the mess and her bed. But the last thing she wanted right now was Myles taking her around and proving to her everything she'd just said. Proving to her how much of a naïve fool she'd been thinking stupid toys made a difference.

'Have you seen the classrooms?' Myles pressed her, not letting her pull her hand free.

Not that she tried too hard.

'No, why?'

He didn't answer as he left the warehouse, locking it quickly behind them, still not letting go of her hand. She told herself she didn't feel the surges of electricity racing through her at his mere touch, making her burn up even though her breath was visible in the freezing night air.

They crossed the compound, away from the hospital and the mess and through the warren of dusty roads to another set of prefab, community-style buildings.

'They have Christmas trees,' she exclaimed in surprise. And over on the other side of the square, a nativity scene had been painstakingly created.

'It *is* Christmas time,' Myles pointed out wryly.

'But it's a *nativity* scene.'

He laughed, but Rae got the feeling it was with her, not *at* her.

'Why not? Just because we're thousands of miles away from home doesn't mean some of the people out here don't have the same Christmas story that we have. They might not celebrate it quite the way we do, with eggnog and turkey, but it's still Christmas. They'll be feasting and dancing and singing.'

'I... Right.' She dipped her head, feeling a little foolish. Myles seemed to understand how places like this worked so easily, whilst she struggled with even the more basic concepts.

'Wait, according to the map the charity drew up for us, the schoolhouse must be around here somewhere.' He glanced around. 'There.'

'Where are you going?'

'Inside.' He barely looked over his shoulder, his voice more a command than a request. 'Come on.'

She'd seen the classrooms through their make-shift windows, complete with mismatched chairs and tables and a very old chalkboard by what had to be the teacher's desk, but she'd never been inside. She hadn't dared.

Rae only paused for a moment before scurrying after him, trying to quell her nerves as he opened the door for her to step inside the deserted building, expecting any moment someone to stop them and tell them that they weren't allowed.

CHAPTER EIGHT

IT WAS THE homemade decorations that struck Rae first. Sparkly paper chains, red felt stockings made from fishing nets, and glittery, colourfully decorated, foam Christmas tree ornaments; red-and-white Father Christmas hats lovingly made from scraps of felt, some well, some not so well, were strewn through the two classrooms. Names she couldn't pronounce sewn haphazardly on each of them with obvious pride.

In a bowl sat ornately carved wooden recorders, ready to be played, whilst an old piano with its missing front and its yellowed keys, hunched yet proud, took pride of place. She leaned over to see what they were learning.

'Those are carols.' Surprise rippled through her. 'Christmas Carols.'

'Probably to entertain the volunteers.' Myles nodded. 'You'll likely be expected to sing along.

'Really?'

'*We* will,' he corrected belatedly. 'Especially when they then teach us some of their songs.

'I didn't know,' she breathed softly.

'You weren't an idiot for wanting to give these kids those toy boxes. They might have to worry about food and water and medical care, but they still love toys and gifts and playing, just like every other kid. Perhaps it can be *more* important out here that they have something like those toy boxes to remind them that they're just kids. That they should still have something approaching a childhood.'

She inched around the classroom taking everything in.

'What are these?' She peered at some cans, empty but for the string lacing through them.

'Shakers.' Myles smiled. 'The kids will fill them with different things, some with grit, some with stone. If food weren't so scarce, they would usually fill some with rice. Then the men will tie them to their legs and do traditional dancing to celebrate the festive season.'

'I look forward to seeing you join in with that.' Maybe it was dangerous, pushing this tentative truce they'd established, but she couldn't seem to help herself.

To her relief he offered a wry smile.

'Fortunately for me, I've been to a place like this before, so I'll have an idea of what I'm doing. But don't think you'll get away without learning the women's dance.'

'Oh, I hadn't considered that. Luckily for me I'm a half-decent dancer. At least I can keep to a beat.' She laughed, realising too late that it might be too reminiscent of that night at the ball.

Was it always going to be this way? Talking with Myles as though she were walking on eggshells, not wanting to say anything to cause him to back away.

He was right, a truce was the most sensible option, and it suited her. She didn't want more than that, of course she didn't. Because that would have been insane.

And yet, once again, Myles surprised her.

'I seem to recall that you're more than a half-decent dancer,' he murmured, his hand reaching out to tuck her grown-out fringe behind her ears.

It was so gentle, so intimate, that she hardly dared to breathe, let alone move.

'Do you like Christmas? Back home?' she whispered.

She seemed to remember he didn't. Wasn't that the reason he'd been so happy to accompany Rafe a decade ago? Because he hadn't had a family of his own with whom he'd wanted to spend the holidays.

'I don't remember the last time I celebrated it. At least, not the way you're thinking. If I wasn't on a tour of duty or some exercise, then I usually volunteered to stay in barracks to cover duties to let the men with families go home.'

Why did she feel compelled to ask him the questions she knew he wouldn't care to answer? What was this urge she had to get to know him? To understand what drove him to be a surgeon? A soldier?

'You don't have a family.'

'Not one I'd care to waste my time going to see.'

At least he wasn't shutting her down outright. Then again, it probably would be wise to let it go.

'Why not?'

He glowered at her, his eyes almost glittering with unspoken distaste. If he'd turned and stalked out of the classroom she wouldn't have been surprised.

Instead, he spoke. Although it was as though every word were being dragged, kicking and screaming, from him.

'My mother gave birth to me, and she just about managed to drag me up. That's about the top and bottom of what she did for me. She had four more kids, Debbie, Ralph, Ally and Mason, all to different men. She was that desperate for love, for a man, that she did stupid things. She was pretty pathetic.'

The accusation sliced through Rae. It was all too horribly familiar. Was that why Myles had been *so* very disgusted by her sex tape? With her?

'What about *your* dad?' she managed to choke out.

'Never knew him. Only Debbie knew her dad, not that it did her much good. Ralph died when he was a baby, cot death. Ally was on drugs by the time she was sixteen. Possibly Mason made it out, but I was gone by then, I'd joined the army, got them to sponsor me through a medical degree.'

'Oh.'

'Wishing you hadn't asked?'

She shook her head but didn't dare answer. Perversely, it felt more like an honour that he'd even told her that much.

'They make your family look like the Waltons.'

'You already met my family,' she countered. 'Aside from Rafe, who grew up with his mum in England when my dad left them for my mum, they're hardly the most…loving people.'

'Love is overrated.' The humourless laugh made her feel sad, as though she wished she could steal away some of his obvious pain.

Pain he would deny if she was foolish enough to try to point it out.

'Is that why you devoted yourself to the army instead?'

His eyes bored into her and, for a long moment, she thought he wasn't going to answer.

'Maybe. And now I'm out and I have nowhere else to go.'

'You could be a surgeon out here, or places like it.'

She shouldn't feel so hopeful. So keen.

'This isn't the life for me.' He shook his head and she felt oddly deflated. 'Not any more.'

'Do you really hate being out here?'

'It brings back memories.'

She didn't know who was more shocked. Her, or Myles himself. Tentatively, she spoke.

'Rafe mentioned that you might be dealing with some level of PTSD.'

She wasn't at all surprised when this time he didn't answer, deflecting instead with a question of his own.

'Do you really love it?'

Despite her disappointment at Myles shutting her out, she found it impossible to stop the smile from cracking her face.

'I do. I didn't expect to, and I know it's only been five days but it feels…good. I feel good.'

'I can see that,' he murmured softly, surprising her.

'You can? I thought perhaps I looked out of my depth?'

'You don't,' he assured her. 'And it isn't just how you appear. It's what people are already saying. Seasoned volunteers who have done multiple medical missions are talking about your skill, your adaptability, your compassion.'

Her skin prickled at his words, making her feel unexpectedly proud. Ten feet tall. So why did the confession come bubbling out of her?

'Sometimes I feel lost. Well…every day, if I'm honest. Back home I might deal with lots of straightforward pregnancies and labours, with a handful of complications thrown in. Here, they're all complicated, and some multiple times over.'

'I know that feeling.' He nodded. 'I found that it worked to approach it a bit at a time, doing a little bit and then another little bit, and then another, until there was nothing left to do.'

'I know. But sometimes that's easier said than done.'

'It's daunting, but you just have to be confident. You need to remember that even if you haven't ever seen any multi-part complications before, you've probably got all the pieces in your head from doing them at different times. Maybe a C-hyst here, or identifying uterine arteries during a bleed there. It's just a matter of putting it all together for one patient, here.'

'I was worried I wasn't good enough. As much as I'm loving it, I'm also finding it a lot harder than being back home. Here almost all the cases are complications, especially obstructed deliveries and UTIs but there's very little for us testwise. There just isn't the equipment to work things up so we have to treat empirically and I'm always hyper aware that if I make the wrong call, if I draw the wrong conclusion—especially since so many of the symptoms could be any number of things until it's too late—the patient can die.'

'Every mortality rate is high out here. Maternal mortality, infant mortality.' He nodded gently. 'It's a fact of life out here that we don't have to worry about the same way back home.'

'Your home or mine?' she joked weakly.

'Both.'

'So I just muddle along, and I try to do the best I can, but I can't help wondering what I'm bringing these kids into.'

'You can't think like that. You just have to know that you're giving mother and baby a better chance than they would have if you weren't there.'

'And being alone can be frightening,' she added after a moment. 'Sometimes exhilarating but sometimes frightening. I'm used to having other obstetricians around me to bounce ideas off, but there are so few of us and so many women in labour that we usually don't have time to stop and discuss cases, or possible diagnoses, or whatever.'

'You're the only one who can decide what to do.' He nodded.

'Exactly. And what if I make the wrong decision? Or hit a vessel? Or—'

'Shh.' He stepped forward abruptly, his hands reaching out for her shoulders. 'You might think you're the only one with these fears but you're not. Everyone is feeling the same but, like you, they just have to get on with it. And like I said before, you're a good doctor, Rae. Everyone values your contribution. What's more, they all like you.'

'Thank you.' Her brain scrambled for words. He was so damned close that her body was going into overdrive. But she couldn't ask the one thing that she really wanted to know.

'Especially me,' he added brusquely.

Almost as though he could read her mind and couldn't help but answer her unspoken question. Even though he hadn't wanted to admit it.

Rae stayed silent, not wanting to break the spell. Not when his hands moved from her shoulders to cup her face, not when his thumb dragged deliciously slowly across her all too sensitive lower lip, not when he lowered his mouth to claim hers with an intensity that thundered through her body and to her core.

He kissed her over and over. Hot and wild and uncompromising. And she couldn't get enough. Standing in that deserted building, clinging onto Myles in much the same way she'd clung onto him the night of the charity gala, and dreaming of doing more—so much more—with this man.

But more of anything with Myles was too dangerous. She knew that. She should pull away now, end things before they went too far.

In the end, however, it was Myles who broke

the moment. His expression was stern but his eyes were still dark with desire, and his voice was too husky, too fractured.

'We can't do this.'

'No,' she agreed, her throat closing up.

He hesitated another moment, then walked them out, wordlessly. The sun was not yet up and their matched strides were the only sound in the silent camp. To Rae, it felt as though they were almost slowing down as they walked, as if each wanting to prolong the time together, yet neither of them prepared to admit it.

And then they were at the door to her room with Myles inching slowly backwards and her standing on the threshold, unable either to put her hand out to stop him or to go inside.

'Myles...that is...would you like a coffee?' It sounded so naked and vulnerable out there that she found herself babbling on. 'It's good coffee. Proper coffee beans. I brought them over with a little hand-held grinder...you know...as my luxury item.'

'Good choice,' he endorsed stiffly, but she noted he took another small step away from her. 'I brought a guitar.'

'Oh...yes... I can imagine you with an electric guitar...'

Like some kind of rock star. It suited Myles perfectly.

'Acoustic actually.' He smiled suddenly. 'The electric sounds better with the amp and stuff, and I didn't fancy lugging all that paraphernalia all this way.'

'Right. Of course. Make sense.'

Abruptly, he glanced up and down the corridor before stepping back towards her, sweeping her inside and closing the door behind them.

'Actually, I think a coffee would be nice.'

The metallic *click* charged through her, as though they were suddenly locked in their very own Faraday cage. It was thrilling and terrifying all at once.

Awkwardly, she moved across the room to make the drinks, moving between the metal cupboard where she kept the beans to the desk where the hand-turned grinder took pride of place. And all the while she didn't dare to turn around, afraid that he'd be right behind her.

Afraid that he wouldn't.

And as she made the coffee and then they sat and made excruciating small talk, she hoped he couldn't read her mind. All she kept thinking of was that moment, back in that classroom, where he'd almost opened up to her. When he'd told her that being out here brought back those memories.

'I'm sorry, you know, that I made you come out here. I didn't know it would be so difficult for you.'

'How could you have?' His tone was clipped but at least he was answering. 'Besides, it wasn't as though you decided to come out here on a whim. You'd already gone through the process with Angela, long before I came along.'

'But when things changed, when Rafe got those death threats and asked you to be my body-guard, I could have explained things to her. Got my mission postponed.'

'Well, it's done now.'

No blame, no censure, just matter of fact.

'I'm still sorry if this is hard for you.' She swallowed, knowing she was risking angering him again, but not able to stop herself. 'There's no shame in talking about what happened...out there, you know.'

The silence was so heavy, so loaded, it seemed to compress the room down. The ticking of the wind-up alarm clock echoed louder and louder, making her heart pound in time to its ominous beat.

Tick. Tock. Tick.

'I understand that.' Myles broke the silence unexpectedly, his tone a little too even, too bright, to be genuine.

As if his head knew it to be the truth, but his soul wasn't entirely in accord.

She waited a little longer but he didn't expand. She hadn't really expected him to.

'So...' she licked her lips '...would you like to? Talk, I mean? I'm a good listener.'

'I'm sure.' He looked at her but she had the distinct impression a part of him didn't even see her. 'But no. Thank you.'

'Myles—'

'How about you tell me about what happened with Justin? And that tape.'

He just about managed to keep the sneer from his mouth.

'I thought you didn't want to hear it?'

'I've changed my mind.'

He was distracting her. She knew that. But he was also offering her a chance to finally give someone her side of events. Someone other than Rafe. Someone who mattered.

Still, she shifted uncomfortably.

'If you don't want to,' he began, but she cut him off.

'I *do* want to. It's just that…it wasn't exactly my finest hour.'

'No, it wasn't.'

Her temper flared and somehow it gave her the impetus she needed.

'Fine, then how about you tell me what you want to know and I'll give you all the gory details to satisfy yourself that I'm as wanton and easy as they like to say I am?'

'I don't want the gory details.' Myles just about kept from snarling. It was madness how he'd spent so many years schooling himself to stay calm in the most incendiary of situations and yet this woman set him off like a match on an oil spill.

'I get the picture, Rae. You got talked into bed by a guy who should have known better than to take advantage of you and during one of your, shall we say, intimate sessions, you decided to film it.'

He had no idea how he managed to act as though it didn't rip his insides out just thinking about her with that sleaze, the man who was supposed to protect her in the aftermath of her high-profile father's death.

'That's exactly what I've been telling you.

There weren't multiple sex sessions. I only slept with him that one time. That was it.'

'You only had sex with the guy once?' He was dubious.

She nodded her head, her body slumping slightly where she stood. Only her hands still on his chest appeared to hold her upright.

'I only had sex with Justin once,' she repeated, coughing awkwardly. 'And the only person I've ever had sex with is Justin.'

'You've only had sex once in your entire life?'

She'd said it earlier, or at least alluded to it, he couldn't remember clearly; his head was still a jumbled mess.

'Ironic, isn't it? Given the reputation the press have given me.'

'You did give them a sex tape.'

He regretted the words the instant they left his mouth. If he could have swallowed them back up then he would have. He didn't even know why he'd said such a cruel thing. If he hadn't known better he might have thought it was jealousy.

But that was impossible.

Wasn't it?

'I'm sorry. That was uncalled for.'

Her woebegone smile only made him feel worse.

'Not entirely inaccurate, though, was it? Of course, my sisters played up to it as soon as they realised they might be able to gain from it, not that we knew it would become something as big as *Life in the Rawl*, and they fed the press all kinds of leads and false stories.'

'Why didn't you object? Why didn't you defend yourself?'

'I was embarrassed. Ashamed. Rafe would have been the only one I could talk to, and, as you already pointed out earlier, he was away on a tour of duty. I had no intention of contacting him. I didn't want him to find out that way. I certainly didn't know soldiers out there—*his* men—had access to it.'

She looked physically ill. It took Myles an inordinate amount of time to process what she was saying.

'So that really was your first time?' he asked eventually.

'Are you listening to me at all?' She scowled at him but eventually nodded her confirmation. 'My first time. My only time.'

'Which brings me back to the question I asked you earlier: why the hell did you film it?'

A look of pain twisted her face.

'I didn't. At least not intentionally. I had no

idea the camera was even there. I trusted Justin. I told you, I thought I loved him. I thought he loved me. He told me he did.'

'He was using you.' Myles did little to disguise his clenched fists.

If the guy had been standing there, in front of him, he wasn't sure he wouldn't simply have knocked him out with a single punch.

'Why the hell didn't you tell me this when we met again in Rafe's offices?'

'Would you have believed me?'

Probably not.

So what had changed?

The fact that she was an incredible, dedicated, focussed doctor, or the way she'd felt in his arms, her body wracked with the climax *he'd* given her?

'Why not tell me that night?'

He didn't have to clarify which night he meant. They both knew. Desire was beginning to move around the room, like molten hot lava threatening to consume her whole. She shifted awkwardly, trying to keep her head, trying not to give into these primal urges that seemed to flood her every time she was with this man.

'What could I say, Myles? That what you did that night was like…nothing I've known before?

I didn't want you to know how inexperienced I was. I felt raw, and exposed, and I didn't want a repeat of that night all those years ago.'

She tried to keep the pain out of her voice but the hoarseness was all too revealing.

'So you rejected me before I could reject you again?'

'I guess.' She chewed her lip and he fought the urge to capture her mouth with his own. 'I spouted all those lies. But you're the one who believed them.'

'I'm not sure I believed them. Not deep down. Not entirely. Not after the way you came apart at my touch.'

'Is that true?' she whispered.

'You were too honest, too giving, too guileless. It was like a completely different person from the manipulative Raevenne of the press.'

Frustration poured through her.

'Then why did you walk out as though you were so repelled by me?'

'Perhaps my disgust was aimed as much at myself as at you. Your brother entrusted you into my care. I was supposed to be protecting you, not taking advantage of you. I was acting no better than that last no-mark bodyguard of yours did.'

Rae stepped towards him, her head swinging

wildly from one side to the other, unable to begin to tell him how many things were wrong with that assessment.

'You're nothing like Justin. *Nothing.* You didn't take advantage of me. I was a gullible and foolish eighteen-year-old back then, wanting to believe the first guy, the only guy, to tell me he loved me.'

'Especially after I'd just made you feel about as desirable as a Christmas sweater knitted by a well-intentioned aunt?' he offered with a touch of guilt.

'I'm not trying to make excuses, Myles. I knew I hadn't imagined the chemistry between us but you seemed to find it so easy to reject me whilst I'd just thrown myself, practically naked, at you.'

'I was trying to do the right thing.'

'I'm beginning to understand that. However, I'm a grown woman now. I might not be experienced but I'm also not imprudent enough to be pushed into things I don't want to do any more.'

Myles raised his eyebrow at her, his dark expression doing little to calm her racing pulse.

'Except when your brother talks you into having a bodyguard you don't want?'

She hesitated, then shrugged her shoulders with as much nonchalance as she could muster.

'Who knows?'

However honest they were being right now with each other, she still wasn't about to tell him that a traitorous part of her had thrilled at the idea of having Myles in such close proximity again. Contrived or not.

Had it been anyone else, would she have capitulated to Rafe's request as easily? Or at all?

She had a feeling her response to her brother would have been curter, more direct, and have culminated in her racing out of there before the doors had even closed to the office suite.

'At least I know I'm not frigid.' She plastered a bright smile onto her lips.

'Say again?'

His dark tone had an edge, a sharpness, which she didn't understand but which dug at her nonetheless.

'That is… Well, I didn't feel like I was,' she stammered. 'I thought I was quite…responsive?'

'Why the hell would you think you were frigid?' Myles demanded.

She wanted the ground to open up right where she stood. A sinkhole that would allow her to escape this new humiliation that she'd brought down on herself.

'Forget I said anything…' she began to plead.

'Did that sleaze call you that?'

What was the matter with her? Drawing attention to all her shortcomings?

'I wasn't exactly…as *responsive* to him as I was with you.' She echoed her earlier words awkwardly.

'Because he couldn't satisfy you he called you names?' Myles was incredulous and, she realised with a start, angry on her behalf.

It was a heady experience.

'It was my first time,' she hedged. 'But that night with you I wasn't as bad.'

'You weren't *bad* at anything. Just as you aren't remotely frigid. He had no right saying that to you.'

'No. But I'm not exactly…' She licked her lips. *What was the opposite of frigid?* 'Not exactly passionate either, am I?'

'Oh, but that's exactly what you are.'

The statement was accompanied with a dark, intense look. Her stomach kicked. Hard.

'Do you need me to prove it to you?'

His words were so low, so loaded. They slid over her skin, into her body, down to her core. She couldn't even answer him.

'I want to hear the words, Raevenne,' he growled.

It seemed to Raevenne that she was summoning all her strength to answer him, yet when she eventually spoke she barely recognised the seductive, sensual invitation in her voice.

'I shouldn't have to beg you to prove anything to me.'

'You just did.' He smirked.

And then he was hauling her to him, her suddenly putty-like body moulding easily against his solid, unyielding one, her arms moving apparently of their own volition to loop around his head, his mouth claiming hers.

Branding her.

His, something whispered through him, *after all this time.*

But he stamped out the sound and told himself this was just about sex. About giving into a temptation that had haunted him for over a decade. It was nothing more than that.

They both understood that it never could be.

CHAPTER NINE

RAW, MASCULINE POWER blasted through Rae, like a towering, cresting wave, and if she didn't learn to ride it, then she would surely end up drowning in it. He was so much. Too much. She felt intoxicated, reckless, lust-fuelled.

The kiss went on for ever, demanding, insistent, unrelenting. Every slide of his tongue against hers made her body pull in and ache for him.

His hand glided smoothly down her spine, caressing her, and making her tremble. When he trailed his touch over her hips she couldn't help but shudder, and when he spanned her waist she stopped breathing.

She thrilled to him. To the way he was taking his time, acquainting himself with every inch of her, stoking a fire inside her that she feared would never burn the same way for anyone else. Never had in the past.

Need pooled within her as her nipples grew

tighter, strained. She pressed herself harder against the wall of his chest as though that could offer her some relief, but it only heightened the ache. Then he was moving his hand around, his palm against her ribs, his thumb grazing the underside of one breast and she was helpless to swallow back the moan that escaped her lips.

'Myles...'

'We have all night,' he murmured.

She shifted against him.

'I don't think I can last that long.'

She shifted as he hooked his fingers under the hem of her tee, pulling it over head and letting it drop...somewhere... Neither of them cared, her bra quickly following. And then his eyes, greedy and dark, were focussed on her naked chest making her rethink the breasts she'd always thought too heavy, too full, to be attractive.

She didn't realise she'd voiced as much until he jerked his head to look at her with an incredulous expression.

'Are you mad, woman? My God, you are incredible,' he breathed.

When he said it, she actually considered it might be true. But when he trailed a finger down the generous valley, cupping a breast in each hand as though testing them, worshipping them, before lowering his head to suck one hard nipple into his clever mouth, she *knew* it to be true.

As his tongue drew lazy swirls over the tight peak, one hand caressed the other, and all Rae could do was drop her head back and arch her body into him, pressing herself into his hands, his mouth. She wanted more, but didn't really know how to go about getting it.

She should *do* something. *Show* Myles how much she wanted him. This time wasn't going to be like the first time when she'd been with Justin, when she hadn't known what she should be doing, hadn't known how to ask for what she wanted.

This was *Myles*. And she knew exactly what she wanted to be doing. *Where* she wanted to feel him. The urge was so deep inside her, as if it was meant to be. As if it was *right*.

Reluctantly, she drew herself back, creating enough of a gap between them that she could divest him of his T-shirt as he'd removed hers. The fact that he let her, that he held himself so still whilst her inexperienced fingers fumbled a few times before succeeding in their task, only helped her to feel more in control. He boosted her confidence without saying a word.

Rae trailed her hands down that incredible

torso, her knuckles deliberately grazing every muscle as they went, enjoying the ride, delighting in every sensation that cascaded through her. Until, at last, she was reaching down between them and feeling for his zipper; then there was the deliciously naughty sound of it sliding open, and the shake of her hand as she carefully eased him out.

He was magnificent, proud, and hot against her palm as she assayed the solid weight of him against her hand, which suddenly felt so very delicate in comparison. As if she could make him believe she knew what she was doing. His low groan of response was guttural, so primal, that she felt it in the apex of her legs, like a Molotov cocktail to her desire.

'Rae...'

Hot need pooled, pulsed, ached, and she heard the sigh that slid of its own volition from her mouth as something pulled tight within her. She moved her fingers up and down his length, revelling in the way it flexed against her, making her feel insanely desirable. Powerful. She coiled her fingers around him, at least as far as she was able, and increased the pressure. Another groan from him reverberated through her, pooling at the apex of her legs.

He grabbed her wrist around the same time he choked out a strangled command.

'Don't tell me that wasn't good,' she offered mildly, as though her heart weren't hammering in her chest for fear of getting it wrong.

'I think you know it was,' his voice rasped over her skin, making it tingle. 'But I want us to take our time, and if you carry on like that, it's going to be over embarrassingly quickly. At least for me.'

A wicked shiver rippled down her spine, bolstering her, making her voice so husky she barely recognised it.

'I think I'd like to see that.'

'I can assure you that *I* would not,' he growled.

He rammed his point home by pinning her arms behind her back, one hand circling her wrists, whilst the other moved back around to cup her breast, to graze his thumb over its straining, aching peak, before lowering his head and drawing it into his mouth. He was playing with her, toying with her. And she, for her part, seemed incapable of doing anything other than arching her back and offering even more of herself to him.

Then, suddenly, his hand was grazing over her abdomen, sliding beneath the waistband, hooking it down. His other hand let go of her wrists so that he could slip off her ballet-style pumps and her soft trousers in one easy movement. And when he grazed his hands back up her legs, his hungry, dark gaze locked with hers, his fingers inching their way up her inner thighs until she could barely keep herself from wriggling on the edge of the desk in anticipation, she stopped breathing, couldn't even remember how to start again.

'Myles...'

And then he was scooping her up, carrying her across the room as she hooked her legs around his hips, his sex pressed, like an iron rod, deliciously against her. She shifted, revelling in his groan, rocking into him, making her objection heard when he lowered her to the bed and moved away.

'Stop grumbling,' he teased, hauling off the rest of both their clothes in a couple of all too slick moves, leaving her naked but, for the first time in her life, not remotely self-conscious.

Instead he made her feel beautiful, desirable, proud. It was an empowering experience, lying there and watching his eyes sharpen with desire as he took her in, his breathing growing shallow and his body...*growing.*

Rae almost giggled, but the sound caught in her throat. For a long moment she could only gawk at him. He was so impossibly hard, like the most revered, chiselled marble sculpture, from his wide, strong shoulders, to his broad chest and athletic torso. Even those muscled, pumped legs. Her fingers ached to touch him, to trace those hard planes and edges, to lower her mouth and taste that tempting skin, but she didn't know where to start.

It didn't matter anyway. Suddenly he had moved down her body, his mouth scorching a trail on the insides of her thighs, working his way higher and higher with deliberate laziness, teasing her, toying with her, heightening her senses.

She found her fingers had worked their way into his hair at some point. Her legs had fallen that little bit wider to welcome his touch. And when he finally skimmed over the centre of her need, she heard the most impossible carnal sound escape her lips.

'Tell me what you like,' he murmured.

'Myles...'

'Tell me.'

'I...like that,' she whispered.

'And this?' He slid his finger through her wet heat, flicking the tiny bud, which had her bucking in response.

'And that,' she confirmed, her voice almost too thick to be her own.

'And this,' he muttered.

And this time she wasn't prepared for him to press his mouth to her core, licking into her, branding her as his. She cried out, possibly an acknowledgement, possibly his name, possibly any number of glorious things, her body helpless to do anything but rock against the perfect rhythm of his tongue, losing herself with every stroke and every suck, feeling herself sinking beneath the waves of lust until they were finally closing in over her head.

When she was writhing in the bed, unable to believe she could take any more of this exquisite torture, he anchored her down with his hands, and feasted on her some more. As though he could never get his fill of her. As though he never wanted to.

Her release came so swiftly, so forcefully, that everything seemed to go black in Rae's head moments before an explosion of colours filled her mind as she cried out his name. She might as well have been catapulting through them, soaring, gliding, with no sign of gravity ever pulling her down again.

But slowly, so slowly, it did, as she came back to herself.

'That was...' She shook her head, searching for the right words but none seemed adequate.

'It's not over yet,' he assured her.

And then he was moving over her, his body coasting slickly over hers, fitting to her as if they were each two perfect parts of a unique, bespoke design. She didn't think, she just reacted, looping her legs around his hips, thrilling in the sensation of his blunt head sliding through her wetness, her hands acquainting themselves with the muscled contours of his arms.

Need poured through her. She recognised it so perfectly, had traced and retraced it almost every night in her dreams since the first time they'd been intimate, but it hadn't remotely compared to the reality of touching him again. Of lowering her lips to his skin. Of tasting him. Salt and sin, maleness and magic.

'Easy,' he murmured as she lifted her hips to press against him.

'It's fine.' Rae slid her hands over his shoulders and down his back. 'I'm ready.'

She didn't know what made her do it—instinct, not experience—but she suddenly twisted her body and lifted her hips again, drawing Myles inside her, gasping as he stretched her, faster and wider than she'd imagined. She had no idea how much self-control it took him but she felt him brace himself, holding himself back, allowing her time to adjust to his size.

'That's why I said easy,' he berated her softly.

She shook her head.

'I didn't realise.'

'No, but I did.' He dropped a kiss onto her forehead, still careful to hold back. 'You can stop frowning now.'

'Am I? Sorry.'

'Does it hurt?'

She wrinkled her nose. It had, for a moment, but not now.

'No,' she confirmed, experimentally rolling her hips.

He groaned and she couldn't help but grin.

'This time, I set the pace,' he warned.

He began moving again, slowly at first, with gentle pressure, sliding himself in and out, a little further each time, his eyes not leaving hers, and it felt to Rae as if she were the most precious thing in the world.

She couldn't have said when the tightness eased completely, she only knew that she had moved her hands lower, gripping him tighter, moving with him as he began to pick up the pace, sliding deeper and harder, their breath mingling as they rode the wave together. Her body lifted up to meet his, to match his, with every perfect thrust. It drove them both on, making need pound through them.

And then her hands dropped lower, clutching at him, pulling him deeper than ever, and this time when he slid inside she shuddered and then she heard his groan of release and everything ignited, like a glorious blaze all around them, consuming them both.

Devouring them alive.

The blow came from out of the blue, pain jolting her awake. As if someone had just body-slammed her to the ground, winding her. Temporarily paralysing her. And then suddenly Myles was growling at her, his tone brutal, dangerous, making her heart pound in her chest with fear even though the words seemed to make no sense.

'Myles? What's going on?' She could hear the rising panic in her voice, but she still couldn't move. She certainly couldn't get up.

It took her another few unnervingly long moments to work out that Myles wasn't really engaging with her at all. And then she realised that he was actually asleep.

Nightmares.

Or night terrors.

The demons of the night that so often came with PTSD.

She'd almost forgotten what her half-brother had told her about Myles' last mission.

Her brain raced. There was a safety protocol associated with this, wasn't there? Something Rafe had once mentioned to her in passing, neither of them ever imagining she'd be in this situation. And that included not waking him whilst he was in this state. At least, not by shaking him awake.

God, what must he be going through? Her chest tightened, and she had to fight every instinct to go to him, to wake up. To stop this nightmare for him.

But that wouldn't work.

Besides, hadn't Rafe once said that some doctors advocated letting the nightmares play out, just managing their effect? Wasn't there a line of thought that suggested that, as long as the individual wasn't a danger to themselves or others, it could be beneficial to allow sleep to play out the fears, to allow the brain to process whatever traumatic event had occurred? Especially if a conscious Myles wouldn't talk about what had happened?

But she needed to get out of the bed. Out of his range. Right now, it seemed, she was too close. He could actually touch her. *Had* touched her, not that he would have realised it. But by being in contact with him she was putting herself slap-bang in the middle of whatever trauma he was reliving right at this moment. And that was pretty much the last place anybody should be.

Carefully, gently, she slid out of the bed and moved away from him. The loss of contact immediately seemed to take the edge away from Myles' actions, although it was clear he was still in some horrible, terrifying world. Her stomach clenched for him.

Would he hear her if she talked to him? Could that help to remind him of where he was? Or at least that he was no longer wherever his mind had taken him?

'Myles,' she murmured quietly. 'Myles, can you hear me?'

She watched the figure but there was no indication that her voice was having any effect. Still, she couldn't leave him like this, not when he was so clearly troubled. She sucked in a steadying breath.

'Myles, it's Rae. Raevenne. Can you hear me? We're at Camp Sceralenar. We're volunteers at a hospital for pregnant women.' Still there was no response. 'You're dreaming. You're safe. Myles, everything is going to be okay.'

She had no idea how long she kept talking, repeating the same things over and over, her voice as quiet and steady and soft as she could make it. Tweaking here, adding there. And slowly, bit by bit, it began to take effect.

Finally—she couldn't have said how much later it was—Myles settled, his sleep becoming more regulated. More relaxed. Deeper. She stopped talking but sat still on her chair in the corner, allowing him to rest. Then, eventually, she stood up, padding slowly around the room as she located her discarded clothing from earlier.

She didn't realise he was awake until she heard him sit up.

'Raevenne?'

She spun around with relief.

'You're okay?'

'Say again?'

He sounded curt. Almost forbidding.

'You were dreaming.' Why was she the one sounding apologetic? 'Well, having a nightmare.'

'Did I hurt you?' He was out of bed and across the room before she could move.

She hated that she couldn't stop herself from taking a step back. Trying to keep some distance between them.

'It doesn't matter.'

He stopped abruptly. Hands that had been reaching out to her dropped to the side with a heavy sound. His expression was heart-rending.

'I hurt you.'

'What were you dreaming about?' she asked.

She knew it was a mistake the moment the question fell from her lips. Even before his body shuttered down.

'I don't remember.'

She should stop now. No good could come from pushing it.

'I think you do,' she said softly. 'And I think you need to talk. Bottling it up can't be helping you.'

'I think I've overstayed my welcome.'

'Myles, please. I want to help. Let me help.'

'I'm leaving. Now.'

She stood immobile, her mind desperately searching for the words that would change his mind; wondering how she could prove to him that she meant what she said. She *wanted* to help.

But his forbidding expression bit into her. An icy shiver rippled down her spine. This was a battle she wasn't going to win.

Wordlessly—helplessly—she dipped her head in acknowledgement as he gathered up his belongings, and left her room.

CHAPTER TEN

MYLES HEFTED ANOTHER crate onto his shoulders and carried it from the four-by-four to the supply room in the compound, his eyes trained on the steady stream of people crossing the river.

He told himself he wasn't brooding. That his head wasn't still stuck back in Rae's room last night. That his mind wasn't still full of her words, her scent, her taste. But mostly, that his heart wasn't full of self-loathing for whatever he'd done to her in his hellish sleep.

He should have known better.

He should never have gone near her, never have let his desire for her overwhelm logic. He was supposed to be looking out for her, not sleeping with her. However undeniable the attraction between them. However intoxicating.

Because, ultimately, where could it ever lead to? What did he have left to offer a woman like Raevenne?

He'd lost his career in the army, he couldn't

function as a surgeon, he didn't even have control over his own head. He was broken. Damaged. Defective.

And she deserved so much better.

He could scarcely believe that last night he had come so astonishingly close to telling her what had happened that last mission. That he had been on the verge of spilling every last regret, and fear, and anguish that had been crowding his head—making him feel as though he was inevitably going to implode at some point—for far too long.

So, instead, Myles concentrated on the tiny figures stretched out for miles on the flat plains on the other side of the river. They travelled fast or slow, in groups or alone, as far as the eye could see. Just like hundreds of thousands of caribou migrating annually across the arctic tundra. Only they weren't wild animals. They were humans. Wretched and frightened, involuntarily displaced from their homes.

His eyes followed the straggling groups as they got closer, became more tightly packed, until they were swarming and grouping, and all desperate to cross the single rope and plank bridge. It was sheer madness how being on one embankment rather than the other would make such an incredible difference to their lives.

In other camps they might be alone because of an earthquake or a flood, or some other kind of natural disaster. But here, over a day's drive from the Camp Sceralenar, the people weren't coming for those reasons. They weren't coming for the women's hospital that Rae ran so smoothly.

He knew what *these* people were running from. Only too well.

For a brief moment, flashes of other images played in his brain like a horror show he never wanted to watch.

He shut them down. But not before he heard Rae's voice in his head telling him there was no shame in talking about it. Logically, he knew she was right. He'd spent the last six months trying to stuff it back down, pretending the memories didn't exist.

And look where that had got him.

'That's the last of it.' Pushing the thoughts from his head, he approached the camp leader. 'Where do you want me now?'

She eyed him up and down with a grin.

'Take a break. Get some water. You must be exhausted. You were like a machine, lifting three crates to everyone else's one. Talk about a man on a mission.'

'I just want to work.' He forced himself to sound pleasant.

There was no need for everyone to know how preoccupied he was. How he wished he weren't here, but back at the main camp. Back near Rae, where he could make sure she was okay. Happy.

Or, at least, happier than he'd made her last night.

What the hell had he been thinking, telling her all that stuff? Things he'd never told anyone else. Never *wanted* to tell anyone else. Because outside the army no one else's opinion of him had ever mattered. Until now.

Until Rae.

He clenched and unclenched his fists at his sides. Why couldn't he get her out of his damned head?

'Well, I'm not going to look a gift horse in the mouth.' The camp leader laughed. 'They're starting to build a couple of new buildings. It's more a matter of putting prefab wooden panels together. Fancy giving us a hand?'

'Not a problem.' He even dredged up a smile. Hard manual graft would be more than welcome. 'Just point me in the right direction.'

'Right around that wall over there.'

He was heading off before she'd even finished talking. Anything to distract him; to help smother the fire he feared was smouldering in him, ready to consume him from the inside out. The embers that he was very much afraid Rae had begun to fan.

Myles looked at the kit, like a flat pack on an enormous scale. The panels were pre-insulated, lightweight and easily assembled, designed to be thrown up quickly to enable rapid erection of refugee camps in times of emergency, especially for geographical disasters like earthquakes or volcanos when rapid reaction times were essential.

He was a few hours into the build when they heard the explosion. For a moment he was sure the very blood had frozen in his veins. He couldn't move, couldn't even breathe.

And then that split-second reaction was over, and Myles was heading for the door, racing out of the compound and towards the noise, his senses taking in everything. Ready to stop, to regroup, if there was any unexpected danger.

And then he rounded the corner.

It was the smell that hit Myles first. The unmistakeable stench of burning flesh. It lodged itself in his nasal passages, reminding him, taunting him. He swayed, momentarily overcome by the flashbacks he'd been trying so hard to thrust aside, dangerously close to reliving that night. His body flushed hot, then cold, the seat making him feel clammy and helpless.

There was screaming and shouting all around him, but experience allowed him to phase it out. He couldn't let cries of pain pierce his emotional armour. Not right now. Not when he was so close to the edge as it was.

Something battered his chest and it took him a moment to realise it was his heart, hammering so fiercely he was convinced it was going to ram its way out. His lungs strained with the effort of trying to draw a breath, desperate to suck in deep lungsful yet struggling to allow in even a trickle. He reached his hand out but the canvas tent offered scant support.

He'd dealt with this before. Too many times, adults and soldiers with devastating, often fatal, burns. But this was a non-combat area, and these were civilians. The tiny kernel of logic that was fighting to make itself heard warned him that it was likely to have been a domestic cooking explosion. It wasn't unusual for a substandard pressure cooker to explode, or for a gas canister, used to make the family meal, to get too close to an open flame.

They might not be used to it in this camp, but he'd seen it too many times over the years.

He glanced around; the chaotic scene in front of him seemed to confirm his suspicions.

And then he saw the child. A young girl with burns on her face and arms and whose leg had clearly been crushed by something landing on her in the explosion. He couldn't tell if she was alive or dead, but if he just focussed on her, if he shut everything else out—the all too familiar cries of pain and pleas for help—maybe he could just deal with her.

Maybe he could save her.

Racing across the room, he dropped to the ground and began to crawl carefully through the debris, his hand reaching out to try to take a pulse.

It was faint but weak, yet even that felt like a powerful victory.

'What's her status?'

A voice dragged him back to reality and he managed to crane his head over his neck enough to see another volunteer, a doctor, had arrived and was trying to get to him. Movement around them suggested other volunteers were trying to reach the other victims. Good, this once he could let others triage, he could just deal with this one child.

This one echo of his past.

'She's alive. Just,' he managed. 'Time is going to be critical. We'll need to get her out to intubate and secure central venous access.'

He had dealt with enough to know that burns victims were usually those who required the most surgical interventions, with multiple trips to Theatre. Not to mention even when burns victims were kids, their surgical procedures were often in line with battlefield trauma surgery usually reserved for adults and soldiers.

'You're a doctor?'

'Army trauma surgeon,' Myles replied automatically, before qualifying it. 'Well, I was up until I left six months ago. That was my last tour of duty.'

This was what he'd been trained for. This was what he knew best. Yet his six months away from the operating table could only have left him rusty. Then again, how many doctors out here with this group would have his particular field of expertise? How many of them would have operated, night and day sometimes, on such cases in such basic environments like this?

The main question was whether the length and intensity of all his operational tours of duty meant that, even rusty, he would still be the best chance this little girl had.

His head was still swirling as the two of them worked quickly and efficiently, clearing enough rubble to get to the girl, who mercifully began to regain consciousness on her own as they worked. Then whilst Myles performed a routine check and pulled her out, the other doctor prepared to intubate, and to take over pain management.

'You have a blood bank?'

'Yes. I'm guessing she's going to need a transfusion.'

'Possibly multiple,' Myles confirmed. 'You're not really geared up for skin grafting here, but we can do something.'

And then his mind clicked over, like turning on a light switch, and the past six months faded away and it was as though he'd never stopped operating. Never stopped thinking about medical solutions.

This was who he was. This was what he had been built to do. How had he forgotten that? But could he begin to separate his army career, which was now over, from his medical career, which didn't have to be?

He'd been an army surgeon for so long, were the two inextricably linked in his mind?

He was so preoccupied with his thoughts that Myles didn't realise they'd been working for almost an hour, and the girl was finally freed, and they were loading her onto a gurney and rushing her into the single, makeshift operating area, where the only surgeon the forward camp had was hastily going over the triage lists.

He checked the girl as quickly as he could.

'Leg's too far gone.' The doctor pulled a sympathetic face. 'We'll have to amputate.'

'She'll be ostracised.' Myles barely recognised his own stiff, raw voice.

A hand appeared on his arm and it took him a moment to realise it was the doctor.

'I'm sorry but we simply don't have the equipment out here, certainly not paediatric.'

'I can do it.'

He heard the words but didn't remember saying them.

'Sorry?'

'I'm a surgeon. Trauma. Ex-army.' Why did it sound so jolted? So staccato? 'I can try something.'

'I thought you were a manual work volunteer?'

'I haven't operated in six months. Ever since I came out.'

'I can't authorise that. Besides, she'll need a skin graft and all sorts.'

'Multiple operations and skin grafts over about a month to six weeks, I would imagine.' He was beginning to warm to it now.

Beginning to feel a little more human.

A little more...*real*.

'Give me some plastic tubes, some wires, maybe some aluminium rods and I can cobble together some kind of external medical scaffolding. A homemade mechanical construction device to realign the bones and hold the leg in the right position.'

'I don't know...'

'Speak to whoever you have to speak to,' Myles commanded, his voice sounding much more like his own. 'Get whatever authorisation you need... *I* need. I can do this. But you amputate without even trying and you've condemned a six-year-old kid for life. You know how harsh their society can be.'

'Yes, but—'

'Starting with early insertion of a subclavian line. Get me an eight-point-five-gauge trauma line.'

* * *

'You didn't say your man was a surgeon, too,' Clara accused jovially as she came on shift to find Rae moving back and forth between two mercifully non-complicated deliveries.

'My man?' She commanded her stomach not to somersault at the idea. There could be little doubt who Clara was talking about.

'Myles, of course.' Clara rolled her eyes. 'Or should I say *Major* Myles? Army trauma surgeon.'

Rae's head snapped up from the chart she was filling out to look at the woman.

'Has something happened?'

'Apparently there was a gas explosion near the forward camp—'

'Was he hurt?' She gripped the edge of the table, her knuckles white with the effort. Relief flooded through her as Clara shook her head.

'Not him. It was in the refugee camp. A couple of families were cooking over a gas stove when the canister exploded.'

'Serious injuries?' She fought to stay focussed, in control, as she glanced between the two mothers in labour, never more grateful for a quiet lull in her shift.

'Multiple.' Clara pulled a face. 'But one of

them was a kid with a crushed leg. The docs there deemed it unsalvageable, and then your Myles stepped up and apparently had some battlefield skills he'd picked up, which enabled him to save the limb.'

'He's not *my* Myles,' Rae muttered. 'Anyway, he operated?'

'Don't know, he didn't come out here as a surgeon so possibly not. But he went into the operating area with one of the surgeons and I'm guessing if he couldn't operate himself then he at least talked the surgeon through it.'

Myles, operating again? Even by proxy, it was a huge step forward.

'So, the kid's okay?'

'They're transferring the casualties here as soon as they're stable, maybe tomorrow. I think someone said the little girl will need more surgeries over the next few weeks, including skin grafts.'

'How do you know this?' Rae stepped forward as she thought one of her mothers might need her, then stopped as the girl was tended to by her mother.

'The other volunteers are back and it's all they can talk about. The mess hall is buzzing. Figured you might want to know.'

'Thanks.' Rae nodded; for the first time since she'd been here she silently cursed the never-abating flow of women ready to give birth.

Maybe when she finished her on-call shift, she could swing by his room.

Maybe.

'Myles...' she knocked tentatively '...are you there?'

Silence, and then, just as she was about to leave, he pushed the door open then backed into the room wordlessly.

The pre-planned teasing quip died on her lips and, in the absence of a verbal invitation, she took that to be the only encouragement she was going to get, and followed.

'I thought you might be asleep.'

It felt like an eternity before he answered.

'I can't sleep. That is... I can't bring myself to.'

'Are you okay?'

She braced herself for him to brush it off. To dismiss her. So it was a surprise when he sat down, his elbows on his knees, his hands clasped between, and his body leaning forward.

'I don't know.'

Carefully, Rae turned the other chair around, sat down, and waited. The quiet swirled around them, almost peaceful.

But opposite her Myles was too silent, too still. As though there were a storm raging in his head that only he could hear. As though it were buffeting him whilst leaving her untouched, only a few feet away.

He looked...*broken*.

'Myles?' She spoke softly. 'What happened?'

For a moment he didn't answer and the silence pressed in on her, far more brutal than the oppressive heat outside.

'You already know what happened,' he ground out when she'd almost given up hope of him speaking to her. 'Or else you wouldn't be here.'

'I came to congratulate you,' she admitted after a moment's hesitation. 'They're calling you a hero out there.'

He made a sound that might have been a bark of laughter but for the fact it was possibly one of the most chilling sounds she'd ever heard.

'A hero is the last thing I am.'

'You saved a little girl. You fought to save her leg when no one else was going to. Out here that's the difference between her having a family to go back to, a home—wherever that may actually be—and being cast out for ever.'

He didn't answer. It was all she could do to resist the urge to pull her chair closer, to run her hands over his bent back, to try to soothe him. To take his pain away.

But she couldn't be that person. She could barely even sort out her own mess of a life, how could she possibly imagine that she could be enough to help someone else?

Besides, Myles would never want her help. Sex was one thing, a simple physical act. But intimacy, actually laying oneself emotionally bare to another person, was a completely different thing. He'd made it clear time and again that he would never want her in that way. She would be a fool to keep repeating the mistake, hoping for a different outcome.

And still, she didn't move.

Which meant she *was* that fool.

So she could scarcely believe it when he started to speak again.

'The smell was almost unbearable.'

He had fastened his hands together, lacing his fingers tightly, around the back of his head, and if she hadn't strained to hear his agonised voice she would have missed what he said.

'What smell?' she asked, tentatively.

'The smell of burning flesh. Once you've smelt it you can never forget it. It scorches itself into your nostrils. Brands itself into your brain. There's no escaping it.'

She wanted to answer, to ease his obvious torment. But what could she possibly say? So instead she waited, her hands balled in her lap to stop her from reaching out to touch him, to comfort him, the way she wanted to. To stop herself from lifting his head to look at her, as though that could somehow break this terrible spell he was under.

But she couldn't risk it. He was only talking now because he was caught up in his own head. If she reminded him of where he was, of the fact that she was there in front of him, he might realise who he was talking to and shut down altogether.

Now, more than ever, she knew how close to the mark her half-brother had been when he'd told her that he thought Myles was suffering.

And so she sat still, quiet, waiting. It felt like an eternity before he spoke again.

'That's what I smell...in those nightmares.'

He lifted his head abruptly, to look at her, to connect with her. And suddenly she wished he hadn't. It was as though something were wrapping itself around her lungs, preventing them from expanding, from drawing in any breath.

The torment that laced his voice was magnified tenfold in that bleak expression, dark torture roiling in his eyes. She wanted him to talk and yet the idea of making him relive it was almost unbearable. She yearned to be the one to take away his pain. To be the one who could make it all right for him.

'From a mission?' she pressed gently, smothering the guilt she felt at knowing more than she was prepared to reveal.

But she wanted it to come from him. She wanted him to be the one to tell her. He dipped his head in what she took to be a nod.

'One of the last missions I went on.' He stopped again, and she held her breath. 'I was on a medical mission, going from village to village treating a number of medical issues. I was looking at a cleft lip, with and without the cleft palate in paediatric cases. There were a few of us, from medics to surgeons, and we had a rifles team with us when we went into the less stable regions.'

She offered an encouraging sound, not wanting to risk speaking and interrupting his thoughts.

'We'd been to a village in the foothills. Whilst I dealt with a couple of surgeries, others tried to resolve some of the more common issues such as diarrhoea and vomiting. There's a general lack of education, poor nutrition, no access to medical care out there. They were mostly farmers so there wasn't a lot to go around, so, other than that, we played some football with the kids and provided some materials and labour to help with general repairs around town.'

'Football.' She risked a soft laugh. 'The universal language.'

Relief coursed through her when it worked.

'Yeah, I guess. Though I'm usually more of a rugby guy, myself.'

She laughed again but didn't push it by saying anything more.

'Anyway, we left the town and went on to the next. A few days later we were heading back to our main army camp when we saw these plumes of black smoke. I don't remember anyone saying anything, but we all knew where it was. Our convoy changed direction and we went to investigate.'

She didn't dare to speak. Not even move.

'When…' He clenched his jaw so tightly, she expected to hear it crack. Shatter. 'When we got there, we saw it. Men, women, children. The enemy forces had been in to kill everyone. And they'd left the bodies where they'd fallen before setting the town alight.'

Hence the smell, Rae realised, forcing herself not to speak.

'We tried to save those few people who were still alive. But it was too late. Plus, we had to go slowly. There was still the fear that some enemy had stayed behind in case we returned, and we didn't know if we were going to come under fire at any time.'

'Which is when Michael McCoy died.'

The words were out before she could stop herself.

He froze as if she'd slapped him. So unmistakeable that she actually had to check herself to make sure that she hadn't.

'Say again?'

Abruptly, Rae wished she hadn't started the conversation. It was as though Myles had the power to control the very air around them. A few minutes ago, she'd been walking out in the hot, dry, dusty camp. Now, it felt as though there were a storm rumbling ominously around the darkened room, a chill tiptoeing over her skin leaving her whole body shuddering.

And yet, she wanted to know. She needed to hear it from Myles himself.

'I heard about Lance Corporal Michael McCoy.'

His jaw tightened. Dark. Lethal.

'Mikey.'

'Sorry?'

'Michael McCoy. Mac, or Mikey, to his friends.' His voice sharpened. 'To me.'

'Right.' She swallowed hard.

'What did you hear? *How* did you hear?'

'Rafe mentioned it. Once,' she added hastily. 'In passing, the night you and I first met at his offices. He said you'd lost a good buddy on that last mission, that you'd taken it hard and that he didn't know the details but he thought you were suffering... PTSD.'

'Is that so?'

It wasn't really an answer. Certainly not the response she'd hoped for. Something tightened around her heart, like an invisible thread pulling it in, painful and constricting.

'I think he thought maybe I could...talk to you. Help you get over it. I'm good at that...listening. Helping people talk.'

Her voice was raw. It made her throat ache.

She might have known he wouldn't answer. Instead, he simply turned the tables on her as though he was the one who deserved answers, not her. The way he always did.

'Is this a game to you?' Without warning, Myles advanced on her. Too big, too powerful, too *everything*. 'A typical Rawlstone Rabble stunt for your own twisted amusement?'

His dark expression should have frightened her. It didn't.

'I don't know what you think you're doing, but I don't want to talk to you about it.'

It took everything she had to stamp down her instinct to object.

She drew in a discreet breath. Then another.

'I understand,' she acknowledged quietly, when her voice was calmer. 'And you don't have to talk. I just wanted you to know that I'm here. If you ever want me.'

'I don't,' he ground out.

But, surprisingly, the rejection didn't hurt her the way she might have expected. With a rush of something she couldn't yet name, or maybe she just didn't want to, Rae realised she trusted him. Perhaps it was because Rafe trusted him, but she didn't think it was that simple. There was something inherently dependable about Myles. Something *she* believed in just as much as her brother did, or, at least, she wanted to.

If only it weren't for that cruel, taunting voice in the back of her head reminding her what had happened the last time she'd trusted a man who wasn't her brother. How her most intimate moments had become public property all because Justin hadn't wanted to give up his grasp on fame.

Maybe if Myles could just give her something, *anything* to show that he needed her. There was more—she knew that...but this felt like a start, a real step forward. She could work on this.

Not that she knew what it was she thought she was working on.

CHAPTER ELEVEN

'WHAT'S THAT FOR?' Myles frowned at the kit bag Rae had just thrown into the back of his four-by-four.

'What does it look like? I'm coming with you.'

Light, breezy, airy. She clearly had no idea how dangerous it was closer to the border. He considered telling her, but then knowing Rae she would only use the information against him later.

'Most of the work up there is sorting out displaced people, triaging medical cases, and administering basic injections that they've never had before, like polio. I can't imagine this camp can spare your expertise.'

'Now that's where you're wrong.' She grinned. 'There are several of us here at the moment, but apparently the forward camp only have two OB-GYNs and one of them has just gone down with a vomiting bug. They asked me if I wanted to go up there for forty-eight hours and take up the slack.'

He felt restless. Frustrated.

'Forget it. They can get someone else.'

'They have me, Myles.'

'Not a chance,' he bit back. 'This camp is so far back it's relatively safe, but the forward camp isn't.'

'Is that a note of concern I hear? I'm touched.'

She was teasing him again. What was more, he *liked* it.

'Don't be,' he growled, his voice far more loaded than he would have liked. 'It's just my job.'

She arched an eyebrow and he wondered how, after last night, he could possibly expect her to believe such a blatant lie. He grunted and stalked around the vehicle and carried out his first parade.

He should regret last night—his weakness in talking to her, in telling her all the things he'd never told anyone before. And yet he couldn't regret it. He'd felt something like relief—he could barely tell, it was such an unfamiliar sensation these days—seeping out of him with every word he'd uttered. As if she were rescuing him from quicksand he'd thought he would be trapped in for ever. Or at least until it pulled him under.

But wasn't that part of the problem? He was

supposed to be the strong one here. He always had been, all through his military and medical career. *He* should have been the one helping *her*. Saving her.

What kind of a man was he that he couldn't look after himself? What did he have to offer a woman like Raevenne?

He glowered at the dusty, barren landscape beyond the compound and offered a bitter laugh. It couldn't have been a more apt vista.

'I want to be with you today.' He startled as she touched his arm gently. He hadn't even noticed her approaching him. 'I thought you might appreciate it, especially when you're talking the other surgeon through the second operation.'

His jaw was so tightly locked he was shocked it didn't crack or crumble under the pressure.

'I'm not totally inept.'

'I never thought you were,' she cried quietly. 'I just wanted to offer you a bit of support. The way you have for me so many times already.'

'You mean, you think I might lose it, after spilling my guts to you last night. You think I might not be able to handle walking someone through this operation.'

'Nonsense,' she snapped. 'I think you'll switch

into the same calm, professional mode you always do and talk them through it flawlessly.'

'Which is why you think I need a chaperone,' he bit out icily.

'Which is why I think you need someone there who knows that you aren't as calm inside as you appear to everyone else,' she corrected. 'You bottle it all up, Myles. That much is clear. And that's what is making your PTSD worse.'

'I don't have PTSD.'

Shame thundered through him at her words, at her assessment of him. He wasn't that man. He wasn't that weak. He refused to be.

And then she placed her hands on his chest, palms flat, rooting him to the ground. He tried to move but he was incapable.

'You have PTSD, Myles. And there's no shame in it. God knows it's understandable after all you've been through. What you had to deal with out there is unimaginable to most people, including me, but you can deal with it. I really believe that. And I believe in you enough to know you can overcome it. But you have to stop feeling as though you're alone in all of this, because you aren't alone.'

He lifted his hands to remove hers. To push her away. Instead, he found himself covering her delicate fists with his own bear claws. She glanced at them, then back up at him, and he would have sworn he saw her eyes glistening.

For him.

As though she really did care.

'There are people you can talk to, Myles. I'm here and I'll always listen but of course I realise you might not want me. Besides, there are those who will understand this better than me. But please, talk to *someone*. The longer you try to ignore it, pretending you're fine, pretending you don't need anyone, the worse it's going to get.'

'You don't know what you're talking about.'

But his words lacked any real bite. The truth was, she made it sound so easy. So appealing. Almost more convincing than the voice in his head telling him to keep quiet. To deal with it himself.

He was out of his depth. Floundering. No one had ever slipped under his skin the way that Rae had. She made him want her; made him *feel* things he hadn't felt in a long time, possibly ever. At least about women. His career had devoured all his time and energy, with the few relationships he'd had sinking because the female in question hadn't understood it. He'd been perfectly okay with that. But now, this one woman made him wonder what he might be missing.

Which was madness.

'We had sex, Rae. It doesn't mean we know each other. It doesn't mean we're suddenly in some kind of a relationship. It was just sex.'

She blanched, just as he'd known she would. Just as he'd intended. But it didn't make him triumphant that he'd made her back off. It just made him guilty. And sad.

Probably because he knew it wasn't true. Sex was one thing. It was a physical, chemical reaction to each other. But what he felt for Rae went beyond that, as ludicrous as it sounded in his own head.

Still, a relationship? Raevenne Rawlstone was the last person in the world with whom he could imagine having a relationship.

Except that he was.

Even if he pushed her out of his thoughts time and again, she crept back into his subconscious. She dominated his dreams. He could still feel the slickness of her skin against his, hear her soft laugh, taste her need. She was wholly intoxicating and he still wanted her.

Right now she was staring at him as though she could see right through him, right into his soul, and she was gathering herself up, squaring her shoulders and readying herself for a fight.

With a start, he realised that she was near livid.

'You think being strong means never leaning on anyone else, always being there for *them*. You think talking to me about what happened to you out there is a sign of weakness. Well, let me tell you this, Major Myles Garrington, you couldn't be more wrong.'

'Raevenne—'

'I bet you you've told this to men time and again. I bet you've even encouraged them to go and speak to someone, a therapist or something. But I bet right now you believe that if you do that, it's you admitting you can't cope.'

'It *is* admitting you can't cope,' he bit out, suddenly.

She snorted scornfully. And loudly. Not even attempting to supress it.

'Of course it isn't. Stuffing it all down and letting it eat at you like some kind of acid from the inside out is weak. Refusing to talk about it when it's clearly killing you is weak. Deliberately putting yourself through night after night of hellish nightmares is weak.'

'You think I *want* to have those nightmares?'

'I think you hate them. I can't imagine anyone would want to live their life in such pain. I think you're a good person who deserved better. But I can't stand by and watch you tough it out as though that's a sign of strength. Please listen to me, Myles, a truly strong man would acknowledge his limitations. A truly strong man wouldn't take the easy way out, stuffing things down, he would make the incredible step of facing his problems, of voicing them.'

He couldn't answer her. Couldn't even begin to get his head around the jumble of emotions crowding him in this moment.

A part of him recognised what she was saying, the same part that so desperately wanted to grab her and hold her and let her ease his pain. But then there was the other part, the monster inside him that taunted and sniped in his ear. Who told him that he had nothing to complain about, given that he had survived when so many of his friends hadn't.

That he'd got off lightly.

That the least he deserved was to suffer a little.

And so he finally found the strength to break free of Rae's touch, and he climbed into the vehicle, started the engine and drove in silence, whilst neither one of them said another word.

But, for the first time he felt cowardly and

alone. As though she was somehow slipping from his grasp and, whatever he tried to do, he couldn't tighten his grip.

How was it possible to lose someone he'd never had?

Rae awoke with a start.

'We've been driving all day?' She glanced at her watch.

'Pretty much.'

Another day down and she was already a fortnight into her month-long mission. It was flying by and she had the oddest sensation that every time she slept she was squandering this incredible experience.

'You should have woken me.'

He didn't deserve the accusation in her tone, but it was out before she could stop it. But Myles, in true form, barely even had to shrug it off.

'You've been on call pretty much twenty-four-seven, since you arrived—all of you OBGYNs have been—so I figured if this was your once chance for some uninterrupted sleep then I was damned well going to let you get it.'

Plus it meant he didn't have to listen to her badger him again. She wrinkled her nose in frustration, but this time kept her mouth firmly shut.

'If you want something to eat, there's something which passes for a lunch in that container over there.'

'Thanks.' Not that she was really very hungry. 'We must be close. Isn't that the Kurkshirgar River? Janine said once the road, such as it is, runs alongside it—we just follow it down to the border camp.'

'Yeah, should be a few clicks further downstream.'

Rae reached for the map, trying to work out where they were in relation to the landscape when the young kid seemed to come out of nowhere, frantically trying to flag down their solitary vehicle.

Her heart thudded as Myles began to slow down.

'You're not supposed to stop anywhere,' she reminded him nervously, glancing surreptitiously around for any signs that they were about to be attacked.

She might have known Myles wouldn't miss what she was doing.

'I've already checked, Raevenne. The ground around is too low, too flat, there's nowhere anyone could be waiting to ambush us here. But would you prefer me to play by the rules and leave the boy here alone?'

She scowled at him, but she could still feel the flush creeping up her neck. She waited impatiently as Myles listened to the boy for what seemed like for ever.

'What's he saying?'

'I think it's his mother. Possibly pregnant, collapsed on the other side of the river.'

Rae's head jerked up.

'Well, how did he get here?'

'I'm guessing the bridge. He mentioned that no one at the camp could help unless his mother got to the bridge herself.'

'If she has collapsed then surely she won't make it.'

Half a statement, half a question. Myles simply shook his head curtly.

'Probably not.'

Rae already knew the answer to her next question, so it was pointless to ask it. Still, she couldn't keep it in.

'There's no way we can drive up there? Cross the bridge?'

'Not a chance. Not going against all those people. It's like a swarm. That's why no one at the forwards camp could. Besides, anyone cross-ing in that direction risks getting shot by bor-der patrols.'

'We can't leave her.'

'No,' he agreed grimly.

'What are you doing?' She hurried after him as he vaulted into the back of the four-by-four and methodically began to open supply boxes.

'Looking for a rope.'

'Why?'

When he didn't answer, she peered around, her mind spinning. The dirty, wide river frothed an-grily as it raced across the land.

Her heart lurched sickeningly.

'Oh…no. You can't possibly be thinking of that.'

'It's the only way.'

She mustn't panic. She *mustn't*.

'That current is far too dangerous.'

'Which is why I'm going to tie the rope around my waist and then attach it to the truck.'

'Myles.'

What else was she to say? How could she possibly convince him that this whole idea was insane? That he was risking his life. That she didn't *want* him to risk his life. Not now. Not ever again.

Because the possibility of losing him hurt too much.

Which was insane, because she didn't even have him to lose. And she never would have.

'Do you want me to help this woman, or not?'

She shot him a look that was anger mixed with pure fear.

'That's not a fair question.'

'Perhaps not, but it's the only question there is.'

Rae stared helplessly, her mind raging as out of control as the torrent in front of her.

'Fine,' she snapped at length. 'But if you're going then I'm coming with you.'

She had no idea how the hell she was supposed to do it. All she knew was that she wouldn't, *couldn't*, let Myles go alone.

She was reaching up and grabbing a second rope for herself when his fingers locked tightly against her wrist, stilling her movement.

'I can't let you do that, Raevenne.'

She pursed her lips, if only to keep them from shaking.

'If you can, then I can.'

He leapt down in one easy movement, coming to stand in front of her, his fingers beneath her chin to tilt her head up. Forcing her to meet his eyes.

'You aren't coming, Rae,' he repeated softly.

She blinked back the hot, prickling sensation behind her eyes, which had no business being there.

'You can't go on your own.'

'I can. Besides, we can't both leave the truck.'

'Myles.'

'Stop, Rae. Just listen to me. This is what's going to happen. I'm going to tie up and get into the back whilst you drive back upstream until I say to stop. Then I'm going to get out and start to cross the river. As the current pulls me downstream the truck will hold me fast. But you keep the engine running and if anyone, *anyone*, approaches you, I'll untie my end of the rope and you'll drive as fast as you can to camp.'

'No!' She wasn't sure if she actually shrieked. 'I won't leave you.'

Was it really possible for a heart to race and hang simultaneously? What Myles was saying was preposterous. If he wasn't tied up, that current would pull him under and smash him against whatever rocks lay on the river bed. His body could end up so far downstream they would never find him.

'Yes, you will. You have to.'

'Myles—'

He cut her off.

'This woman needs our help, Rae. This kid needs our help. So I'm going to cross and you're going to stay with the truck.'

'And wait for you to get back?'

'No, just until I've crossed. Then I'm going to release the rope and you're going drive to camp. Just like if someone approaches you.'

She opened her mouth to object but he pre-empted her.

'And the longer you argue, the less chance his mother has.'

'But, Myles…'

'Get a team and wait for me at the bridge. If I can get her down to you, I will.'

'And if you can't. If the baby is coming?'

'Then I'll try to deliver it. I watched you enough times in your clinic, I can make a decent attempt. I might not be you but if I'm all she has then I'm better than nothing.'

She wanted to say *no*, but part of her knew it could be the only chance this woman had.

'What about the boy? You can't take him with you—it's too dangerous.'

'Far too dangerous,' Myles agreed.

'And I'm not supposed to take him in the truck, but I can't leave him here.'

'I don't think you'll have a choice.' Myles jerked his head to where the kid was fixed on the river bank. 'I don't think he'll leave this spot as long as his mother is on the other side. He knows what I'm trying to do.'

'Will he be safe?'

'Safe is relative in these parts,' Myles offered grimly before putting his hands on the tailgate to jump back in. 'Okay, I'm tied up. Take us back upstream.'

Rae saw the boy before she saw Myles.

She'd been pacing the compound for several hours when she saw the kid heading down the road, his face as pinched and frightened as before. But whilst his body had been stooped with desperation before, it was now straighter, taller, more hopeful.

He was keeping a steady pace, but this time there was no shouting, no drawing attention of any kind. Still, his eyes were trained across the river, and Rae could only follow his gaze, something which might possibly have been her stomach lodged in the vicinity of her throat.

Myles.

His gait was unmistakeable, although he had shirked the volunteer garb that he'd been wearing in favour of something closer to the clothing worn by the people swarming across the bridge. And in his arms, the unmistakeable figure of a pregnant woman, a bundle in her arms that, Rae realised with a jolt, looked suspiciously like a newborn baby.

There was clearly an issue.

It felt like an age as he reached the bridge, joining the throng who were already jostling to cross the narrow planks. She could see him moving, trying to fight his way through. All she could do was wait, and pace, knowing that every minute was crucial to the baby and the mother, but unable to do a single thing about it.

And then he was close enough for her to call a couple of local volunteers to bring out a gurney, which arrived at the same time that Myles did. There was no missing the blood covering the woman's clothing, and Myles'.

'You delivered the baby but the mother's haemorrhaging?'

'Yes. There was no choice, that baby was coming out. The heartbeat was weak but it was there, I had to clear its lungs and nose of fluid. It will need to come back with us to the neonatal team. However, it's the mother I'm most concerned about. She hasn't delivered the placenta and now she's haemorrhaging.'

'Okay, let's get her inside and check her levels. I'm guessing her haemoglobin is going to be down so we'll need to find her some blood—her son would be a good start—and start transfusing her. Then we can get inside and try to get that placenta out.'

CHAPTER TWELVE

'YOU'RE VERY QUIET.'

They were almost an hour into the drive back to Camp Sceralenar, the ambulances with the more urgent patients in the convoy, but the two of them alone again in the four-by-four.

She hitched her shoulders, her gaze fixed out of the window.

'You can talk to me, you know.'

'I know.' She smiled sadly but didn't pull her eyes away from the barren landscape. 'I just don't know what to say.'

'There was nothing you could have done, Rae. The baby was born too early and they just don't have the equipment out here to help these babies survive. But you saved the mother. Because of you, the kid who flagged us down isn't an orphan right now.'

'I know that.' She turned her head slowly to look at him.

'It just doesn't help,' he supplied.

'No, it doesn't. I just… I'm not sure how I feel.' She drew in a long breath. 'When I first arrived here I was shocked at how brusque people were. How cold. How little they grieved, or showed their grief. They were so desensitised to all the death and I couldn't understand it. Now I think I do.'

Was the tight coil inside his chest normal? Like an over-wound clock.

'Do you?'

She shrugged again.

'One in five foetuses don't survive here. That number is so much lower back home, and those that don't survive are often lost well before labour. I might see one death a month. But out here I see them every day. Multiple times. Worse, most of those babies die because of complications during labour.'

'There's no care out here,' he concurred quietly. 'Most of these women don't even know there's a problem until it's too late. And even if they did, what can they do about it? There are so few hospitals, and anyway, what money do they have?'

'Exactly.'

He could see her swallow, desperately trying to hold herself together.

'I couldn't understand how they could be so accepting, so stoic, at first. But these women go into pregnancy knowing the chances of something going wrong are high so they are prepared to lose their baby. Perhaps too prepared.'

'Probably,' he concurred, 'but there's nothing you can do to change that. That's the way life out here is. You just have to find a way to deal with it. To cope.'

'Like you have.' She cast him a sidelong glance before looking away guiltily. 'I'm sorry, I didn't mean that.'

'Yes, you did. In your own way.'

But he was astounded to find that it didn't rankle as it had in the past. It didn't grate on him. He *wanted* to talk to her. To let her into his head. To help her to know him, to *understand* him.

As if he believed she could actually *help* him.

He'd lost his career, his reputation, the life he'd known. The only thing he had left to give her was his honour. Then it was up to her. She could take him, or she could leave him. His chest constricted painfully.

He'd battled terrible enemies, been in firefights that should only ever have had one outcome, lost too many friends to count. He told himself he'd withstood worse than any woman walking out on him, then ignored the little voice that goaded him that Raevenne wasn't just *any woman*.

'And you're right, I haven't found a way to deal with it so I've just been bottling it up inside. But it was always bound to spill over at some point.'

He was aware she'd stilled. She was frozen in her seat wanting neither to look away nor to engage, for fear of breaking the moment. For a few moments, he turned his head from the road and met her clear, direct gaze whilst something rolled through him, low and unstoppable, like a drumbeat, or thunder.

'I'm grateful to you for offering to be the one to listen, but I need you to know that I'm not making any promises. I can't guarantee that I'll be able to tell you everything, or that it will make any difference.'

'I don't need anything from you. I just want you to know that you have that option,' she whispered.

He nodded, unmoving for another moment, finally turning his attention back to the road.

'Part of the reason for not wanting to talk about the night…that we found the village burning… was that I was trying to protect someone.'

He didn't realise he'd stopped talking until Rae spoke up hesitantly.

'Lance Corporal Michael McCoy?'

'No.' He shook his head but then stopped again. When she reached her hand out to touch him, her fingers resting gently on his forearm, it was oddly encouraging.

'I was trying to protect his daughter.'

'His daughter?'

'Kelly. She was five years old and she was his whole world.'

Rae sucked in a breath, sympathetic but still not understanding. He didn't blame her.

'A few days before that mission Mikey had received a letter from home. A well-intentioned family member telling him that they'd discovered his wife had been having an affair.'

Her hands fluttered against her throat, a shocked sound escaping her lips.

'They wrote a letter? When Mikey was in a warzone?'

'They meant well. I guess they thought he was better finding out with his friends around him than coming back home to his wife knowing nothing about it.'

'God,' she breathed. 'What an impossible

choice. But surely… I mean, why did they put him on that mission?'

Guilt, black and familiar, erupted through him like molten lava in a volcano. She gasped, horrified.

'I'm so sorry. That was a stupid thing to say. I didn't mean it at all how it sounded.'

'His OC thought he was okay.' His voice was raw, fractured, barely recognisable. 'When I mentioned my reservations to him, he said that he'd known Mikey a long time and that he was confident. I couldn't argue. I tried telling Mikey he should sit this one out but he begged me not to push it. He explained that he already knew about the affair, that he'd confronted her about it after we'd come back from our previous tour of duty, but she'd sworn it was over.'

'Oh, Myles. What a horrible choice to have to make.'

'He told me it wasn't news to him, that he'd been handling it just fine all this time whilst the rest of his squad knew about it. I couldn't put my finger on why I wasn't so sure, so I let it go. We were days away from the end of his third tour and his rifles squad had been protecting my medical team for eight months. We'd been lucky enough to be together from the start of this tour without any significant casualties, and he didn't want to dip out on the last mission of the tour.'

'He made it sound so plausible.' Rae exhaled.

'He did, and I believed him. With hindsight, I should have known better. The other guys saw what they wanted to see, whilst I was just far removed enough to see the warning signs for what they were. But it was a standard recce and we didn't expect to see anything significant out there so I made the decision to keep his secret. It's a decision I will regret for the rest of my life.'

His voice cracked and for a moment, he couldn't speak.

'What happened, Myles?' Rae prompted softly, and he actually believed she could feel every last drop of his anguish. 'What did Lance... What did *Mikey* do?'

It was as though a dense, black fog had descended over him and he couldn't see, couldn't breathe. Still, he forced himself to push through it.

'We walked through that village, looking for survivors, the stench and the sights worse than any kind of horror film anyone could ever make. I still can't be sure exactly what triggered him,' he began, 'but suddenly he just lost it.'

'Lost it?'

Something roared through Myles, as though trying to drown out the words he didn't want to say.

'He knew they had to still be somewhere in the area. They weren't hard to track. We tried to stop him but… I've never seen anyone move so fast, as though the horror of it had taken him over. We heard the firefight even as we raced in but it was too late.'

He stopped the vehicle, unable to trust himself; needing to step out for a moment, to let the cool night air flow over his skin, to quell the nausea churning his stomach into a quagmire of regret and recrimination.

Wordlessly, Rae got out of the vehicle and moved around it until she was standing in front of him. He had no idea how long they stayed there; it could have been hours, or maybe merely minutes. Then, abruptly, she bowed her head so that her forehead was resting against his, cool and settling. Neither of them moved, barely even breathed, but eventually, *eventually*, the roaring in his head began to abate.

'None of us have ever voiced it, but I can't be the only one to think that Mikey must have known what the outcome would be. That he couldn't have hoped to take them all on alone. That he…didn't intend to come back from it.'

Rae raised her hands to cup his face.

'It wasn't your fault.'

'I should have told someone I thought he wasn't up to it. I should have fought harder to make people listen.'

'You said it yourself, they already knew but they chose to see what they wanted to see. A strong Mikey, not one who was hurting.'

The vision of her swam in front of his eyes.

'You think that makes it easier?'

'I'm not sure anything will make it easier.' She jerked her head lightly from side to side. 'Your responsibility and loyalty to the men you were so close to is strong. I think you'll always believe there must have been something you could have done. Even if there wasn't.'

'You don't understand. It was *my* job to anticipate all of that. If I had insisted on dropping him from the recce, he'd still be alive. A five-year-old girl would still have her father.'

'That's not realistic. And I think you know that, deep down. You did as much as you could with the information you had at the time. Odds are, if you'd left him behind on that mission, you'd have come back to find he'd found another way to do it. Rafe told me a few soldiers couldn't take any more and took their lives in the toilet blocks on camps.'

He couldn't deny it.

'And if Mikey had done that,' she continued sadly, 'you'd have been beating yourself up for *not* taking him on that mission. Thinking that if you had, he would still be alive.'

In the darkest recesses of his head he'd wondered the same thing, too many times to recall, over the years. He'd woken up in a cold sweat, his mind searching to touch an answer that could never be found. He held his head up, his voice sharper than he intended. But at least it didn't break or splinter, the way he felt his very soul was doing.

'We'll never know.'

And that was the worst part about it.

His words hung between them, like a shimmering, electrically charged barrier.

His guilt was palpable. Perhaps he was most guilty that the surgeries he'd carried out on those villagers had drawn the attention of the enemy, made them collaborators. Maybe it was more about Mikey. Probably it was a combination of the two.

She gazed at him, as though silently willing

him to keep going, and not to suddenly regret his frankness, and shut her out instead. He hated the sorrow in her expression, almost as much as he hated that flicker of hopefulness behind it. As if she imagined him opening up to her now meant so much more.

Because he couldn't guarantee her more. He couldn't guarantee her anything. He was damaged. Worthless.

'Is that why you walked out on the army? The surgeries? Because you think this is the punishment you deserve?' she asked suddenly.

'You say it like you don't believe it.' He couldn't keep the accusation out of his tone. 'You think it's right that those innocent villagers should die, that I let one man get to the point where he took his own life, that one little girl now has no father, and all the while I get to walk away unscathed? To walk around as though nothing ever happened?'

'But you aren't unscathed, are you?' she pointed out. 'You don't walk around as though nothing happened. You've sacrificed everything: your career as an army officer, your career as a surgeon, even some kind of a decent life. You can't tell me that taking a job as a bodyguard to the vile Raevenne Rawlstone wasn't your idea of punishment.'

'You're not vile.' Anger coursed through him without warning. How dared she talk about herself that way? How dared she even think it?

Rae held her ground.

'But you didn't know that at the time, did you? You thought I was vacuous, and trampy, and spoilt. The perfect penance for someone as culpable and selfish as you?'

The blackness swirled faster, harder.

'You're not that woman.'

'And you're not that man,' she declared triumphantly.

His eyes seared. Scalding and furious. He practically spat the words out at her.

'You don't know what you're talking about.'

'Except that I do,' she announced, ignoring his attempts to intimidate her. 'I've got to know you now. And even if I didn't, my brother knows you, yet he gave you this job. He entrusted me to you.'

She lifted her hands to his chest. The way she had only a few nights ago. Reminding him all too easily of how it had been between them. How it maybe could still be.

'He trusts me. But I don't deserve that trust.'

'You absolutely do. And that's why I trust you, too.'

He couldn't stop himself. He covered her hand with his, his calloused thumb pad caressing her skin.

Less than a month ago he'd thought she was like some kind of breathtakingly beautiful angel, but that it was only skin deep. But he'd been wrong. She was beautiful inside, as well as out-side.

He'd spent the last few weeks humping and dumping. He'd hoped that working out here would soothe his battered sense of self-worth and it made him feel as if he was starting to heal. As if he could be useful again. Worthy.

Worthy of Rae?

He thrust away the taunting voice but he wasn't quick enough. New questions tumbled around his head.

Could he ever be worthy of a woman like her? She was incredible, blending in seamlessly, with no trace of the socialite he'd thought he'd known. She was like a different version of herself out here. A better version. Freer. More comfortable in her skin. The *real* Rae, he realised abruptly.

A woman he could easily fall for.

The thought was like a lasso around his chest. Tight. Constricting. That could *never* happen. Because even if Rae wasn't the woman he'd believed her to be, he was still the man he knew himself to be.

Lost. Anchorless. Valueless.

He had nothing to offer a woman like Rae. He was damaged, and not just physically. He'd lost his body and he'd lost his career, but more than that he'd lost his reputation. His only worth now was in the work he could do in places like this. Here he felt so much more. *Here he felt whole.*

He didn't belong back in regular civilian life— coming out here had proved that much to him. There was no place for him back there. There was no place for him in Rae's world.

It should have made him want to back away from her all the more. Instead, it made him want to grab hold of the woman he had, enjoy her for the here and now. She'd be gone, moving on from his life, soon enough. The thought terrified him.

Gripping her wrists, he pushed her away from him.

'Confession over,' he bit out as coldly, as icily, as he could. 'We're expected back in camp and you're due on shift in a couple of hours. You don't want to let them down, and start living up to your old reputation, do you?'

And as she flinched he told himself the shattering in his chest was triumph.

CHAPTER THIRTEEN

'YOU'RE GOING TO need to sterilise her if you perform a Caesarean section on her,' Janine, the senior consultant, murmured. 'If it's her third C-section, her uterus will be severely weakened.'

'I know, but I don't see another option for her,' Rae concluded dully, glancing across the room at the patient in question. As if things couldn't get any worse, the girl was on oxygen, still not even stable, and although they'd succeeded in bringing her blood pressure down significantly, it was still elevated. 'Not if we're to save her baby.'

There were times when Rae could feel her limitations pressing in on her, constricting and cruel, but the truth of it, Rae realised with something close to contentment, was that there was absolutely nowhere else she would rather be. She might not have known it three and a half weeks ago when she'd first driven into the camp, but this was where she was meant to be in her life.

In places like this, helping women who might otherwise have had nothing.

Perhaps not for ever, but certainly for the foreseeable future. As much as she'd loved her job in her New York practice, it simply didn't compare to how proud, how fulfilled, and, yes, how permanently exhausted she felt out here.

It almost made up for the way things had taken a sour turn with Myles. She'd thought that Myles opening up to her would be a turning point, bringing them closer together, maybe even allowing them to take their physical relationship to another level. One where they could possibly consider actually *calling* it something of a relationship.

She couldn't have been more wrong. Unfamiliar bitterness trickled down her spine.

It was as though talking to her the way he had that night, opening himself up to her and showing her his vulnerabilities, had actually made him push her away all the harder. They'd barely spoken since that day, even before he'd volunteered to return to the forward camp for forty-eight-hour shifts, on two more occasions since.

Folding her arms over her chest and straightening her spine, Rae told herself that she didn't care. Hadn't she told herself years ago that the only person she could rely on to make her happy was herself? Not her family, not her friends, not a man.

And certainly no other man would do for her now that she'd been with Myles. He'd ruined her for life; she knew it for a fact. No one else would ever, *could* ever, come close.

But she had medicine, her career, and that was going to be enough.

More than enough, she chanted brightly, turning her attention back to her immediate patient.

The twenty-seven-year-old woman had come in with such severe pre-eclampsia that her skin had split in some areas and was at high risk of infection. They had battled to reduce her blood pressure, and stabilise her baby's condition and, for a while, it had seemed to work. But now the baby's health was beginning to deteriorate again. They had to get it out.

A third C-section meant a third scar, leaving the girl's uterus too vulnerable to risk further pregnancies, which meant sterilisation was going to be the safest course of action. It wasn't going across well with the young woman, or her family, who were beginning to turn on the interpreter.

'I'd better get in there and support him.' Rae started across the room. 'This was my other patient I've been keeping an eye on. She came in pregnant with twins and fully dilated. She's with the midwives but she's been pushing for quite some time now, and I think we might need to help things along by delivering the first baby with a vacuum.'

'I'm on it.' Janine nodded. 'You just go and deal with your pre-eclampsia patient.'

'Thanks,' called Rae, already hurrying across the room to where the husband was standing apart from the family, his face etched more with concern than with anger.

Instinctively, Rae summoned the interpreter over, a young man by the name of Lulwar. Her voice was low until she could be sure her suspicions were correct.

'Can you ask the husband what he's thinking?'

The two men spoke briefly, quietly, the family too emotional to notice.

'He wants to know, if this happens, then his wife will be safe?'

'Yes. She won't be able to have any more children, but there's a good chance that any further pregnancies could end up life-threatening for his wife.'

She watched the husband's face as the interpreter passed on the information. Relief pouring through her when he bobbed his head in acknowledgement before a look of determination settled over his features as he stepped forward, silenced the arguing family, and took his wife's hand.

Rae grabbed a local nurse quickly.

'Can you go and secure me the next OR please? Emergency C-section and sterilisation.'

And after that the patients, and the obstructed deliveries, kept coming. And by the time her shift was over, it was all she could do to drag herself to her room and flop down into her bed, asleep somewhere before her body even landed on the mattress.

Tomorrow would be Christmas Day which meant that her month-long mission was nearly over. It also meant that it was the first Christmas she hadn't spent with her family throughout her entire life.

She was almost sad to realise that with the exception of Rafe she didn't miss them, or their inevitable dramas, one little bit.

'Happy Christmas, Raevenne.' His low voice only just carried the couple of feet between them.

Rae swung around, startled, peering into the

shadow of the building where he'd been watching her for some time.

'Oh, I didn't see you there. Right. Yes. Happy Christmas.'

She didn't look particularly overjoyed to see him. If anything she looked wary, not that he could really blame her. He'd been avoiding her ever since the drive back to camp when he'd laid himself out there. Logically he knew that it wasn't her fault he'd felt vulnerable, and weak, but that hadn't stopped him from taking it out on her, by avoiding any real contact, ever since.

Mainly because he knew the instant he saw her every regret and reservation he had about talking to her would melt away, replaced instead by the ache to draw her to him, kiss her thoroughly and pretend that none of the bad stuff, none of the baggage, even existed.

'I heard you performed some really impressive procedures over the last few days.'

'Oh?'

'Not least a heterotopic pregnancy.'

He could practically read the internal battle she was waging in every flicker of her expression and he had to fight not to smile. It was typical *heart-on-sleeve* Rae fashion. Or was it just that he knew her better than either of them would probably care to admit?

'Let me guess,' he drawled. 'The private part of you wants to tell me where to shove it, whilst the professional part of you is so geared up by the medical stuff that you're desperate to talk about it.'

She scowled at him. Or she tried to, anyway.

'You can't just flip-flop like this, Myles,' she muttered.

'I know.'

'You open up to me, let me into your most private moments one minute, but the next you're acting as though I barely even exist.'

'I accept that.'

'And now you're pretending nothing even happened.'

'You're right, and I'm sorry.'

He didn't know what he'd expected her to do, but it wasn't to narrow her eyes at him.

'Of course you are. Until the next time.'

Something scraped inside him. He hated the way she was looking at him. As if he wasn't to be trusted. As if he wasn't even someone she liked.

'I wasn't going to tell you this until we had everything squared away and everything accounted for, but we think we've caught the company responsible for the death threats, Rafe's brakes, and your break-in. They're a rival company who lost out on a bid to your brother about a year ago.'

She didn't even blink.

'I know.'

'You do?'

'Rafe emailed a few days ago.'

She was giving nothing away.

'I see.' Myles dipped his head, fighting back some alien emotion pushing within him.

'Rafe also said you'd been working flat out on the investigation even from out here.'

He shrugged.

'I did what I could.'

'Why?' He hated that her voice was so brittle. 'For me? Because you owed Rafe? To appease your own conscience?'

And then he looked at her, and it finally hit him. He understood what it was that had made her fight so hard to distance herself from *Life in the Rawl*, why she'd been so averse to having another bodyguard, why she'd felt compelled to volunteer for a mission like this.

'They really did a number on you, didn't they?'

Rae stopped. Her attempt at nonchalance betrayed by the way her breath had caught in her throat.

'Who did?'

'Your sisters.' He lifted his shoulders. 'Justin. The press.'

'I can handle them.'

She jutted her chin out a fraction, her voice apparently as airy as ever. She looked magnificent and proud, and...something else besides. Something quite different. He'd been watching her closely long enough now to begin to be able to read her, from the way the pretty flush deepened slightly and crept down her neck, to the way she was shifting, almost imperceptibly, from one foot to the other.

And so he knew magnificent and proud were only a part of it. There was another side to her, and it was fragile, vulnerable.

It was amazing that he hadn't spotted it before. That no one else had spotted it before. Or perhaps people just didn't want to. They preferred the more heinous version of Raevenne Rawlstone, so that was what they believed.

The question was, why had she let them?

'I know you can handle them, but the point is that you don't want to keep having to, do you? It won't matter to them how many good deeds you do, they're going to want to write the lies, because juicy scandal sells papers, not charity work.'

'It doesn't matter.' She flashed a smile, which he now recognised to be too practised, too tight to be real. That realisation gave him a kick. 'I don't care what they write, anyway.'

'Up until a month ago, I used to believe that.' He didn't deliberately soften his voice, it seemed to just…happen.

'And now you believe differently?' The question was almost off-hand, as though his answer didn't matter to her either way.

But she'd hesitated a fraction too long.

'You truly love being out here, don't you?'

She didn't meet his gaze immediately, and when she did look at his face, he got the impression she was staring at a point just on his ear, rather than looking at him directly. As if a part of her was guilty for her answer.

'I find it very…rewarding.'

Surely it didn't actually *hurt* him that she felt she couldn't be honest?

'If they asked you to return for a three-month stint, would you?'

He couldn't explain why his heart was hammering so hard. And then her eyes flickered to his, just for an instant, and she pursed her lips.

It was as though someone had dealt him a blow that had punched every bit of oxygen from his lungs.

'They've already asked you, haven't they?'

'Yes.'

'And you agreed?'

'I told them I would consider it,' she hedged.

'But you intend to agree.'

It wasn't a question and she didn't answer it as though it had been one. But working out here had been a good move for her, both professionally and personally. She suited this life. She was good at it. She felt fulfilled by it. That much was obvious.

'I don't see any reason why I shouldn't come back.' Her voice sounded odd, as though she was challenging him. 'Do you?'

And all at once he wanted to grab her and tell her that there *was* a reason. That he wanted her in his life. That when they got home maybe they could start again, perhaps see if they could have a future together.

But then he looked into those laurel-green depths and saw everything that she loved was out here. How could he ask her to leave that behind? How could he ask her to leave herself behind? Especially when she'd only just worked out who she really was.

'You're right, you *should* come back,' he said slowly, realising that he meant it. 'Either here or somewhere else. You can be yourself here, without the media constantly hounding you and fabricating stories about you.'

'I'm not running away.' She jerked her head sharply.

'I never thought you were. But you have so much to offer, both as a doctor and as a human being. And the press won't let you do that. They want to pigeonhole you because it suits their agenda to do so. Out here, you can be the person that I think you've always been meant to be.'

'Really?' Her shy smile abraded against his hollow chest, and he pretended he didn't see the confusing hint of sadness in it.

Just as he pretended that he didn't feel Rae everywhere. Restoring feeling to his body after it had been growing cold for so long. Making him feel alive.

Which left him with a choice. He could continue punishing her for little more than being the one person he had trusted enough to open up to. Or he could set aside all the reasons why being with her was a bad idea, and why it could only end up hurting one or both of them, and he could just enjoy this one perfect day with her. *Christmas* Day.

'Have you eaten yet?'

She blinked slowly at him.

'Not yet. I was just heading over there now.'

'May I join you?'

She slid him a pointed look, her tone dark.

'And if I said *no*?'

'*Are* you saying *no*?'

He refused to bite and after a long moment she sighed, a little overly dramatically for his tastes.

'I should. But this place is too cramped to avoid each other indefinitely. Besides,' she added loftily, 'it *is* Christmas.'

A smile toyed at the corners of her mouth and he had to fight the impulse to kiss it away. This was exactly what Rae did to him. She chased all logical thought, all sense of self-preservation, from his head until it was filled with only one thing. *Her.*

She made him want to tell her all the deep, black thoughts that crept around his head in the still of the night. She made him want to find a way to cage them so that they no longer plagued him. She made him want to be a better person.

But what did he really have to offer her?

He'd been a good soldier, a brilliant surgeon. Now he was neither. Neither of them had anything to rush home for, yet whilst Rae consequently couldn't wait to get back to another place like this, he couldn't wait to get out of here. But where even *was* home for him?

At least that answered his question, then. He had *nothing* to offer her.

And yet here he still was. Unable to stay away from her any longer. Wanting to spend this day in her company. They were on borrowed time, he and Rae, and he should know better. But right here, right now, he didn't care.

'It is indeed Christmas,' he agreed. 'So let's go and feast.'

It was a Christmas beyond all she could have hoped for. The men dancing, rice cans attached to their legs, their feet practically a blur as women kept time with sticks on the ground. At one point she was even hauled to her feet by some of the women and challenged to match the rhythm; faster and harder and more complex all the time.

It was exhilarating, and incredible, and special.

Not least when Myles looked over from where his own group was taking part in the festivities, the glance they shared so intimate. So unabashed.

Then the refugees sang traditional songs, and when it came time for the volunteers to share their own carols, something akin to pure joy suffused Rae as she turned to find Myles standing there, right next to her.

And then he smiled, and a memory—a decade and a half old—rushed her.

She was in love with him.

All over again. She wanted more with him. She needed more. But if she couldn't help him to face his demons then there was never going to be a chance for them.

Sliding her hand into his, Rae waited for a moment until they could slip out unnoticed, the festivities finally winding down, and led him to her room.

There was no easy way to tell him so she just plunged in.

'I—I've been doing some research into your case,' she announced, trying to ignore the shake in her voice.

'Is that so?'

'It is.' She swallowed hard. 'And I've found out that they think that village was attacked by the local forces in retaliation for the villagers selling some of their harvest that year, instead of saving it all for the rebel soldiers.'

'I see.'

'Which means it wasn't about you or your team. It wasn't because you were there helping people.'

She'd never heard of it at first, but it turned out it was pretty commonplace—farming villages whose crops should have easily provided enough food for themselves and for sale at market, but who were on the brink of starvation because each season almost all their crop was taken by the warlords.

But she knew that didn't mean Myles was about to accept her word for it.

'I have letters, research, if you want it.'

'I've already heard about it. It was a theory.' His clipped tone was clearly intended to end the conversation.

She couldn't give up that easily.

'Whose theory?'

'It doesn't matter.'

'It does to me.'

A month ago his glower would have cut into her. Instead, she found herself sitting up straighter, maintaining eye contact. She had started this. She had to see it through.

'Myles, please... I want to understand.'

'An army theory.'

'You don't believe it?'

Disappointment shot through her but she wasn't prepared for his answer.

'I...don't know. I didn't back then. It felt as though it was an easy answer to salve my conscience. But now, with the benefit of time, of distance, of *you*, then maybe.'

It was like a church full of perfectly pitched choirboys all singing beautifully in her head all at once.

It didn't mean Myles accepted what had happened. But it did at least mean that he was open to possibilities.

'So what does that mean?' she breathed, scarcely willing to break whatever spell they were under.

His fingers laced through hers, his perfect turquoise-sea eyes not leaving her face.

'I can't make you any promises, Rae, but maybe we can just try to enjoy these last few days together—not that work will give us much chance—and see how it goes from there.'

It wasn't declarations of love, but it was better than anything she could have hoped for.

'I wish I had bought you a Christmas present.'

'The only Christmas present I want is you, in my bed,' he murmured, his body tightening as her gaze grew hotter, more intense.

She lifted herself up onto her toes, her breath tickling his ear as she leaned in to whisper to him.

'That's a Christmas present I can give very freely.'

CHAPTER FOURTEEN

'RAE, OVER HERE.'

'Raevenne, sweetie, this way.'

'Give us a quick smile, Rae.'

Rae flinched as the photojournalists crowded in on them even as she stepped around the arrivals gate at JFK airport.

Relief warred with regret when Myles slipped instantly out of the intimate atmosphere that had enhanced their last few days together, working hard and playing harder, and back into bodyguard mode.

'Your *fame*?' he asked grimly.

She pulled a face.

'It has to be. Nothing is private, not even going out there to do charity work.'

It made her all the more grateful that she'd already accepted another medical mission— a three-month stint, this time—and would be headed back out before Easter. She couldn't get away from this circus fast enough.

Sticking as close as she could to Myles' impressive body, with which she'd finally become more than familiar, and with which she intended to reacquaint herself as soon as they got to her home, she allowed him to plough a path through the melee, and out of the main doors. The car waiting for them was mercifully in sight, although the press weren't letting her go without a chase.

'Can you tell your fans how it was at Camp Sceralenar?'

'Did you save any lives, Rae?'

'Were you aware that your bodyguard is a British army hero? That he risked his life climbing down a hillside in enemy territory to retrieve the corpse of a Lance Corporal Michael McCoy, who had taken his own life?'

Rae froze, dropping back for a moment as she turned to try to see who had made the last comment. She wasn't prepared for Myles to practically drag her off her feet and to the car.

'Keep moving,' he bit out. 'And don't engage.'

'Did you know that when McCoy defied orders and instigated a firefight with the enemy, resulting in his own death and the injury of several of his squad, Major Garrington told his commanding officers that he was culpable just so that McCoy's young daughter Kelly wouldn't find out that her father died dishonourably?'

She could practically feel the fury rolling off Myles' body, his muscles tense and bunched. She prayed no reporters came too close. But Myles restrained himself, his focus on getting them both to the vehicle.

In a daze, she allowed herself to be bundled inside, pushed across the soft leather seats, her bergens taken off her and the door slammed on the baying pack outside. In slow motion she turned around, watching Myles throw the luggage into the boot of the car and stalk around to climb in the other side.

And then the car was pulling away and the silence might as well have been hemming her in.

She ran her tongue around her mouth. My God, she was so stupid.

'Myles—'

'Forget it.'

It was an icy warning, which she should have heeded. But she couldn't. Desperation clawed inside her.

'You can't really be blaming me for this?'

'I've never told anyone else that information about Mikey's family. Only you.'

'This is the press.' She flung her hands up.

'They unearth all kinds of stuff if they're so in-clined.'

His stark look was excruciating.

'No, Rae. You did this.'

'No.'

Her shoulders slumped but she refused to look away from that glare; she would not let him think she was guilty.

'Yes. You engineered it.'

'You can't really believe that.' Pain and disap-pointment lanced through her.

'You wanted the press to know. All this time you've been acting like you moved away from your reality life, but what was the truth, Rae-venne? That you got pushed out for not repeat-ing that bit of TV gold and you've been looking for a way back in ever since?'

'Of course not.' Horror spread through her like wildfire. 'I don't care what they think. Not any more. I only cared what Rafe knew. What *I* knew. What *you* knew.'

'And yet you couldn't let it go. You had to re-lease the story. And now they're running sto-ries about my career, about my missions, about Mikey.'

He didn't mention little Kelly. He didn't need to. She felt sick with the knowledge.

'I didn't say anything, Myles. I never would.'

'I don't believe you.'

Every word, every accusation, was like a lashing to her already broken soul. But still, she made herself lift her chin. She forced herself to meet his eye.

'I can't make you believe me. But I know the truth. Just as I know that part of the reason you want to hate me now is because you don't know what else to do with the emotions you stuff inside you and never allow to come out. Emotions which are eating you from the inside, Myles.'

'You don't know what you're talking about.'

'I do. And I didn't do this, but I can't say I'm unhappy the press have found out. Because it's time you stopped blaming yourself for what happened. Being an army trauma surgeon has been your life for so long that somewhere along the line it became what defined you, and when you lost that part of who you were, you lost yourself.'

The words shouldn't have penetrated his fury or his misery. Nothing should have.

And yet they did.

Suddenly, he saw the hurt and misery in her expression. He realised he was the one who had put them there. Even as the knowledge snatched his breath away, it wasn't enough to change what she'd done.

The signs for the railway station couldn't have come at a more fortuitous moment.

'I can't do this with you, Raevenne. Or, more to the point, I *won't*. Everything is always drama with your lot and I've seen enough drama to last me several lifetimes.'

'No, Myles—'

'Stop the car, please,' he ordered the driver, before turning to his side and taking one last look at her. 'I'm sorry, Rae. We're done.'

CHAPTER FIFTEEN

RAE PULLED THE baby out, blue, floppy and covered in thick meconium-stained amniotic fluid. If she was going to help it transition to life outside the room she was going to have to work quickly. But, as ever, resources were limited and she had to act fast.

Picking the baby up, she transferred it quickly to the resus table using an Ambu bag to push air into the limp baby's lungs, but the meconium was filling the mouth and lungs, stopping the chest from rising. She checked the pulse.

Decelerating—just as she'd feared.

'Cath, can you grab an aspirator and start getting this meconium out? And just ask someone to see if Janine is still free? The mother is haemorrhaging.'

She didn't wait for an answer, watching instead as her colleague began to clear the baby's airways.

'Okay, that might do it.' Rae nodded after what

felt like a lifetime. For the baby, it so easily could be. 'Let's try again.'

She didn't realise she'd been holding her breath until she pushed more air into the baby's lungs and finally, *finally*, heard the faintest of whispers. It wasn't much, but it was better than nothing.

Still, when she turned to the new mother to see her staring over and, despite her own pain, tears of relief spilling freely out at the miraculous sound, Rae felt her own heart swell with pride.

She really did have the best job in the world, she realised, handing the baby over to the mother whose arms were already outstretched. Even out here, where resources were scarce, and maternal and infant mortality was so high, there was still the pure joy of hearing a baby cry for the first time.

It almost made up for the fact that, in order to have this life, this career, she'd lost Myles.

Less than a week after she'd watched him go, a ringing sound had already built up in her ears. Part of her had been desperate to run after him, a bigger part of her had been too paralysed to move. She had almost welcomed the numbness that had been beginning to settle over her, because at least that acted as something of an anaesthetic against the pain she recalled all too vividly from the last time Myles had rejected her.

The ringing had grown louder and more insistent. With a start, Rae had realised it wasn't in her head after all, but her mobile, and she'd heard Angela on the line telling her the next replacement medic had dropped out, and inviting her to jump on a return flight.

She'd opened her mouth to decline, to say that she couldn't possibly return without Myles. But the words hadn't come out. They'd lodged in her throat. And then she'd caught herself.

Myles had gone. She'd had nothing to lose. And besides, she'd loved operating out there, and feeling she was making a real difference. At least she would have that, even if he wasn't with her to share it.

The next thing she'd heard was her own voice accepting Angela's offer.

Could it really only have been five days ago?

It felt like an eternity.

Either way it was time to get over any secret hopes she'd harboured that Myles might step back into her life. Time to accept that he was now well and truly gone. Since he and Rafe had uncovered the source of the death threats there was no reason for Myles to return. She didn't need him now.

At least, not as her bodyguard.

But in the emotional sense?

If these past few days had taught her anything it had reinforced the fact that she loved him. She always would. He had her heart in a way no other man would ever have. Because no other man came close to matching Major Myles Garrington. And that was okay. Some people went through their whole lives without meeting their soulmate. But she had.

And that month she'd had with Myles was hers for ever. She could hug it to herself and no one would ever be able to take it away from her.

'You're done?' Janine barely lifted her head from attending to the haemorrhaging.

'You need some help?'

'No, but the new general surgeon arrived this morning. I was going to walk them through a procedure out here when you called.'

'Shall I take over here so you can get back to her?'

She still couldn't see Janine's face, but she could hear something colouring her expression. If Rae hadn't known better, she might have thought it was excitement mingled with amusement.

'No, I'm happy with this. Besides, might be fun for you to do the walk-through.'

Rae wrinkled her nose, wondering what she could possibly be missing. But there was no time to dwell. Leaving the bay, she quickly scrubbed up and darted around the curtain to the operating area, a bright, welcoming smile on her lips.

'I'm Rae, sorry we have to meet under these circumstances, but hopefully we'll get some time later. How can I help?'

'Apparently you're going to help me identify the uterine arteries.' A pair of all too familiar eyes met hers.

Her heart hung, time seemingly slowing around her. He couldn't be healed, not in a week. And yet he was out here, and apparently the new general surgeon.

'Myles...?'

'Indeed.'

'General Surgeon?'

'I wanted to move away from what I did before. And it isn't as though I didn't do lots of other trauma cases over the years. But maybe we can discuss it later. Before my patient bleeds out internally,' Myles prompted, but there was no mistaking the expression in his gaze.

It promised her all the explanations she could want. Afterwards.

The one that told her everything was going to be okay. He'd healed himself, and he'd come back for her.

Everything else could wait.

Twenty hours, six C-sections, and a slew of both complicated and non-complicated deliveries later and they were in his tiny room, each with a fresh, hot coffee.

She waited for him to start the conversation, afraid to speak first.

'I love you.'

She froze. Her body might as well have stopped working. She stopped swallowing, stopped blinking, stopped breathing.

Something welled inside her and she had the sudden, frightening suspicion that it was the urge to say the words back to him.

But she mustn't.

A much as hearing him say he loved her was like the most beautiful song in the world piped straight into her chest, she needed more than that. She needed to understand.

'I admit to a level of combat PTSD. You were right. I already knew it but I couldn't bring myself to admit it aloud before now. Perhaps a fear of looking weak, or maybe a fear of losing respect. I certainly lost my self-respect. I didn't know who I was, caught between the army soldier I'd been and this new, terrifying life on Civvy Street.'

'But you're still the same strong, responsible man you always were,' she managed. 'Anyone can see that.'

'*I* couldn't. Not until I met you. You helped me to see that I had a problem, and that I needed to talk about it.'

'And did you?' she whispered.

'Did I talk to someone? Yes. I went to see my old brigadier.'

She stared at him, winded.

'When?'

'After I left you in the car, outside the railway station. When I went into the station there was already a train ready to leave so I bought a ticket and I jumped on board. To this day I don't know where it was headed to. I realised my mistake a couple of hours in, disembarked at the next station and made that phone call to my old unit.'

His wry smile tugged at her. 'You didn't make the entire journey?'

* * *

Myles shook his head.

Guilt scraped away inside him. He'd been so caught up in his own internal battles that he'd wilfully ignored the war that Rae, too, had been waging. She loved him. Just as, he realised with a heavy thud, he loved her.

He was *in* love with her.

He had been pulling the whole macho soldier routine and toughing it out, but even though it had fooled almost everybody else, it hadn't fooled her.

He loved her. A deep, fierce, strong love, which he'd never known he had the capacity to feel, before now. But that also meant recognising that he had nothing to offer her, that he was a shell of a human, and a fraction of the man he used to be. He'd been an army trauma surgeon for so long that he didn't know how to be anything else. Which meant that he was nothing. He was damaged and broken, and Raevenne deserved so much better than that.

And something had begun to untwist inside him.

He'd been existing. But he hadn't been living.

And then he'd met up with Rae after all those years.

A woman who seemed to turn the lights back on in his life. She poured warmth—*life*—into even the bleakest, coldest corner.

'Bit by bit, these past couple of months, you helped me deal with a pain I'd been pretending I wasn't wallowing in. You began to save me that month we spent out here last time. But it was time for me to start saving myself.'

For himself as much as for her.

He owed them both that much.

She deserved someone who could give her so much more than he could offer right now. But as that old, familiar, lost grit began to burn inside him again, Myles knew that he was ready to stand back up, to fight, to be the kind of man worthy of a woman like Raevenne Rawlstone.

He had one more shot at living. He wasn't going to mess this one up.

'So what did you talk about with your brigadier?'

'Too many things to explain now. Old missions. Old buddies. Guys who are no longer here. It wouldn't make sense to you if I told you now. It wouldn't…mean anything to you. But, if you like, over time, I can tell you the stories. Even introduce you to some of the old guys.'

A part of her wanted that, *wanted* to talk to people who knew another side of Myles. But then she thought of her brother, and how closely he guarded some of his stories. Things he knew that she could never fully understand if she hadn't been out there with him.

'That's okay.' She placed her hand on his chest instinctively. 'That's your past. Your memories. Keep them precious. I want your future.'

'And you have it,' he told her fiercely. 'I can't promise that the nightmares are over. Or that I won't have lapses. But I know who I am now, with you, and I know that I can overcome them. I can't control everything, not with the villagers or with Mikey. Or with you.'

'Oh, I don't know about that.' She blushed naughtily, thinking of the nights together when his unique set of skills had controlled her body most efficiently.

The difference was, she was beginning to learn that she had her own set of skills to control his body, too.

'I'm here for you, though,' she added seriously. 'Whenever you want me. To talk to, to distract, or even just to hold.'

'And I promise you, I'll always come to you from now on. I'll never push you away again.'

'I like the sound of that,' she murmured, pushing him down on the bed and moving to sit astride him. 'Starting from now?'

'From now.' He dipped his head in agreement.

'Prove it,' she murmured, lowering her mouth to his.

'Shh… Listen!' He grinned suddenly.

'Ten…nine…eight…seven…'

'Myles?' she blinked, mumbling against his hot, vaguely salty chest.

'…six…five…four…'

Abruptly, she sat up, finally hearing the muted chanting outside.

'Three…' she chorused quietly with him, her hands resting on his shoulders as she straddled him and felt him begin to grow hard already. 'Two…one… Happy New Year!'

'Happy New Year, Rae.' He lifted up to claim her mouth, his hands gliding up and down her spine to cup her backside. 'Maybe we should make those promises New Year's resolutions?'

'I don't care what you call them,' she moaned gently, 'as long as you honour them.'

'Oh, I will. Trust me.'

And then he obliged, more than happy to begin showing her all the ways he intended to make good on his promises.

For the rest of their lives.

* * * * *

LET'S TALK

Romance

For exclusive extracts, competitions and special offers, find us online:

f facebook.com/millsandboon

◉ @millsandboonuk

🐦 @millsandboon

Or get in touch on 0844 844 1351*

For all the latest titles coming soon, visit millsandboon.co.uk/nextmonth

*Calls cost 7p per minute plus your phone company's price per minute access charge

Want even more
ROMANCE?

Join our bookclub today!

'Mills & Boon books, the perfect way to escape for an hour or so.'

Miss W. Dyer

'Excellent service, promptly delivered and very good subscription choices.'

Miss A. Pearson

'You get fantastic special offers and the chance to get books before they hit the shops'

Mrs V. Hall

Visit millsandbook.co.uk/Bookclub and save on brand new books.

MILLS & BOON